Night
Swimming

Also by Pete Fromm

Night
Swimming

Stories

Pete Fromm

Picador USA
New York

Several of the stories reprinted here appeared originally, in somewhat different form, in the following publications: "How All This Started" in *American Fiction* 9 (fall 1997); "Night Swimming," under the title "A Splash of Red," in *Witness* (November 1998); "The Investigator" in *Glimmer Train* 15 (May 1995); "Black Tie and Blue Jeans" in *American Way* (August 1, 1997); "Willowy-Wisps" in *Passages North* 16 (Summer 1995); "Doors," under the title "Raising Robert," in *Good Housekeeping* (January 1998); "Wind" in *Owen Wister Review* (April 1998); "The Thatch Weave" in *The Crescent Review* (Summer 1999).

Design by Ellen R. Sasahara

Library of Congress Cataloging-in-Publication Data
Fromm, Pete.
    Night swimming : stories / Pete Fromm.—1st Picador USA ed.
        p.   cm.
    ISBN 0-312-20936-3
    1. United States—Social life and customs—20th century Fiction.
I. Title.
PS3556.R5942N5   1999   99-22213
813'.54—dc21   CIP

First Picador USA Edition: September 1999

10   9   8   7   6   5   4   3   2   1

Rootie-toot-tootie, another beauty
for DeGrootie.

Contents

Night Swimming

How All This Started

Without a word of warning my sister Abilene jumped out of her crouch, shaking her gun at me. "Piss on this, Austin," she said. "What good's a gun if you can't shoot anything?" Then she was off and running.

I tore after her as best I could, holding my own gun out to keep the willows from lashing my face. I barely made the truck before she roared off. With her last year of high school almost over, I was forever trying to keep her in sight, not let her leave without me.

Holding on to the door handle with one hand and the fraying seat belt end with the other, I glanced over my shoulder at the red tornado we kicked up in our wake. That was always my favorite part of driving off the roads with Abilene—that furious rush of Texas dust and dirt.

Catching me looking, she shouted, "No moss on our backs!"

I loosened my grip and asked, "Where we going, Ab'lene?"

"The river," she said, bouncing us through a hole that launched me into the roof of the cab, driving the button on top of my cap into my skull. I grabbed the door again, trying to hang on, but clamped my other hand over my head, hissing at the eye-watering stab of pain.

Still barreling along, Abilene took a hand from the wheel and reached under my cap, rubbing at the sting. "Sorry," she said, smiling.

I was never big on asking Abilene a lot of questions. I didn't say a word the day she cut the seat belts out of her truck, saying, "No moss," with each rip of her razor knife. But this time, maybe because of the way she was rubbing my head, I said, "How come the river?"

"What's the hardest thing you can think to shoot?"

"Doves," I said right away, what we'd been hiding in the willows waiting for before Abilene jumped up that way. I pictured their herky-jerky flight, the teardrop-bullet shape of their whistling bodies. I'd picked up whole boxes of empty shells to carry home with only one, maybe two birds.

"Nope," she said, leaving me to guess.

I waited a minute to see if she'd help, but she just kept rocketing along. "Quail?" I asked. "The popcorn kind?" That's what she called the ones that pop straight up and fly every which way.

"Nope," she said, so fast I knew I wasn't supposed to get it.

"Think, Austin! Not just what people hunt. Anything, anything at all. What would be the hardest?"

"I don't know," I said, but she still wouldn't help.

I was about to say "People?" just for something to say, when she said, "Swallows," grabbing the wheel tight, slithering through the turn and bucking down the ruts to the river. "Think of trying to hit one of them."

How All This Started

Bodies the size of gnats, I thought, picturing them flitting up, down, left, right—wherever the bugs flew. Later she'd take me out to try to shoot bats, but this time I thought she had it. There couldn't be anything harder than swallows. They lived all along the river, in mud nests stuck right to the cliffs. Now, at dusk, with the bugs coming out, there were swarms of them zinging around. They weren't afraid of us. Sometimes they'd come so close I'd duck.

Abilene said, "First one wins," and she fired before I thought she was serious. She missed and before long we were both blazing away, piles of empties growing around us.

When we took a break I rubbed at my shoulder, my ears buzzing. Abilene stared down at the empties, like all of a sudden this wasn't much fun anymore. "Austin," she said, "do you think this is crazy?"

"What?" I asked.

"This. Everything." She waved her arms around. "Do you think I'm crazy?"

I couldn't think of a way to answer so I didn't say anything, just stood there watching the smile grow across her face.

"Thanks," she said, throwing her gun back up and firing, as if I had given her some sort of answer.

I hit the first swallow. Not the one I was aiming at, but one flying behind and above mine. Zigged when he should have zagged. He crashed on the shore and I stared at him. "I win," I said, before I saw how Abilene was looking at me.

"You weren't aiming at that one," she snapped.

The way she said it I answered, "I know," as quick as I could. "Was just luck."

"No slop," she said. "Nobody's won anything yet."

We kept shooting, but after that I only aimed enough to miss, afraid I might hit another by accident. Since she'd started acting this way—the troubles, Mom and Dad called it—I didn't like beating her at anything, though I was twelve now, old enough I sometimes almost had a chance.

Finally it was nearly too dark to see and the swallows were going back to their nests anyway. We stopped shooting, but Abilene loaded another five shells into her gun. "Want to know the secret?" she said. "The swallow-killing secret?"

I didn't say that I did, but Abilene said, "Hit 'em where they live."

She didn't even lift the gun, but shot from the hip, straight across the river at the cliff crowded with mud nests; all five shots as fast as she could work the pump. I covered my face with my hands as the BBs sang back around us. After the fifth shot I looked up and though it was dark I could see the big vacant holes where the nests used to be. The birds were in the air again, circling everywhere, back and forth, peep-peeping.

Reflecting the last of the day, the river was glossy and as I turned to follow Abilene I saw the little dark spots on its surface, the floating bodies of the dead swallows that didn't reflect anything.

I hopped into the truck beside Abilene, and as she spun it around to point back up the bluff, I said, "You got a pile of them, Ab'lene."

"I know," she said. "I win."

We started going out for swallows pretty often and after a while we got good enough we could hit them on the wing now and then and Abilene never shot the nests again. She still didn't think we were hitting them often enough, but she said she had a plan for that.

Before we went out the next time Abilene took my gun, which was really Dad's, and clamped it into the vise. "What are you going to do?" I whispered. She was rummaging around in the toolbox and I moved so I was standing between her and the gun.

"Here," she said, pulling out a rusty hacksaw. "We're going to make the ultimate swallow gun."

"Don't, Ab'lene," I said, sliding out of her way when she kept coming. "Remember when you cut the stock?"

She'd done that when I was only ten, so the gun would fit into my shoulder. And though Dad hadn't used it in years he went through the roof when he saw it. "Who on earth do you think you are?" he asked Abilene.

Abilene leaned tight to him, peering up into his face. "We could hardly bust it out of its cobwebs!" she shouted. "Time for you to pass it on and get the hell out of our way. That's what fathers do."

That was the first time she ever really shouted at him, and Dad stopped in the middle of what he was saying. Big and tall as he was, he only looked like some giant tree, just before Paul Bunyan yells timber. He pressed his lips together, not exactly the way he did when he was mad, and stared at Abilene. Then he turned around and we almost didn't hear him say, "I wish I'd never seen Abilene."

He meant the city, not my sister. See, my dad's favorite story was about how we got our names. Not where we were born, but where we were conceived. "How all this started," he'd always say, waving his arms around him like he had a kingdom to show off. He'd tell the story to anybody who asked, and some that didn't. Made most people blush or change the subject. As huge as Dad was, and Mom so tiny, Abilene was always saying it must have been a freaking freak show. After she told me about The Facts, I could hardly believe we'd been born in the first place. The very thought grossed out Abilene and me.

At first whenever he'd start, me and Abilene would leave the room. Then, as Abilene got older, she'd ask things to make him look bad, things like, "What would've happened if Austin came first? Would you have called him Abilene?"

He'd look at her, confused, then try to remember where he'd been before she interrupted. If he couldn't remember he'd just start over at the beginning. "We were young, newlyweds, and you know what that's like. We were just in Abilene for the night." I could picture his every smile and grin, always coming at the same parts. Abilene said the whole story was so much lizard shit. She said, "I bet we were adopted. God, I hope we were."

She sawed more than a foot off the barrel and we got tons of swallows, shooting down low along the river, where they cruised for bugs hatching out of the water. The shot scattered all over out of the short barrel and if you waited right you could knock down three, four, five at a time. Nobody ever said Abilene didn't know what she was doing.

One night we got so many she had me collect them. Wading out in the warm water I tossed them back to shore where Abilene gutted them. After bringing in the last of the birds, I sat down next to her. The swallows were so tiny Abilene had to scoop with just her pinkie and I wondered if maybe she really was crazy. "What are we going to do with them?" I asked.

"Have them for dinner. Deep-fry them in olive oil. I read about it. They do it all the time."

I looked at her. "Who?"

"Italians."

"Italians?" I said.

When we came into the house Mom and Dad were standing in the kitchen and Abilene leaned both our guns against the wall in plain sight. I followed her in with my arms full of swallows. "Look," I said, hoping Dad wouldn't notice the sawed gun. Mom and Dad stared at all the tiny, naked birds, each one smaller than a golf ball. The meat was dark, dark red, almost purple. "I'm cooking tonight," Abilene announced.

When Mom started to say something Abilene shushed her. "Austin," she said, "get me the fryer." To Mom and Dad she said, "Go on into the living room and relax. This is going to be an experience. Most excitement for you guys since that night in Abilene, or maybe Austin." She gave me a whack when she said that, rolling her eyes to the ceiling.

Dad, I noticed, was looking at his old shotgun, at the hacked-off barrel, even the splinters at the end of the stock still visible, though that sawing was a few years old by then. It'd be tiny now in his big hands. He looked over at Abilene and back at the gun. He must have felt Mom staring at him and he glanced her way before stepping to the guns, his shoulders sagging. He picked up Abilene's first and jacked out all the shells. Then he picked up his old gun and did the same. He put all the shells in the big pockets of his pants. Leaning his gun back against the wall he said out loud, "I was so proud when I first got this."

Abilene snorted.

"Come on, Ruby," he said to Mom and they walked quietly to the living room.

For a while now if Mom and Dad tried to get her to act

7

any certain way Abilene'd start screaming, "Please, please, please, tell me about Abilene again, Daddy! Tell me How All This Started!" She'd wave her arms to show what she wanted to know about—all of us, our whole lives. Mom and Dad hadn't been able to figure out anything to do but walk away.

We didn't have any olive oil so Abilene used Crisco. "There's not an Italian within a thousand miles of here anyway," she said. When the swallows were done she loaded them onto plates, heaping Dad's so high they kept falling off. She called them to dinner and we sat around the table staring at our swallows. Dad made the first move, poking at one with his fork, trying to pull some meat away from the tiny bones.

"No, Daddy," Abilene said, and I could see Dad's fingers whiten around his fork. "Like this," she said when he looked at her. She popped a whole bird into her mouth with a suddenness that made me flinch. I could hear the crunching as she chewed, then she swallowed and smiled. "Scrumptious."

I was the next to try. It was kind of fun and the bones weren't much more than sardines'. Abilene tossed one into the air, calling, "Peep, peep," before catching it in her mouth. She winked at Mom.

Mom scraped her chair back and went to her room.

Dad stayed with us though, and eventually he put a swallow in his mouth and slowly bit down. He chewed and said, "These are good, Abilene. Really."

Abilene winked at him, too.

Dad said, "Maybe we ought to do more of this. Trying new things."

"Well," Abilene said, "with that new swallow slayer we'll be steady on swallows for a while, but I think it's going to open a lot of doors for us."

She was pointing right at the mutilated shotgun and I shrank back in my chair, but Dad just nodded and reached for another swallow.

Later that night, when I was in bed, another fight blew up downstairs. I couldn't make out many words, but when I crept out to the top of the steps I heard Mom's voice, as thin and fragile as she was, pleading, "But Abilene, it's for your own good. We worry about you."

Abilene laughed like crazy at that. Then she stopped, chopping the laugh out of herself with a crash, something metal against something wood. I could hear Mom suck in a startled breath. I pictured her standing there, her hand halfway to her mouth, trembling, even her bones thin, like the swallows', ready to crack and crumble. Abilene shouted, "Don't ever call me that filthy name again! Never! I'm Abby."

"That's fine, Abby, honey," Mom said.

Abilene shrieked, "My name is not Abby-honey!"

I wondered how Mom had gotten the word Abby out so fast, so natural. It was the first time my sister had ever mentioned it as her name.

Abilene thundered up the stairs then, carrying the gun she'd sawed off. I thought of the slam of wood against metal and figured she must have swatted the gun against the table to get their attention. I crouched against the hard, turned posts of the railing and though I was in plain sight, Abilene marched right past. The bang of her door made me wonder if she hadn't pulled the trigger.

I waited but Mom and Dad didn't come after her and pretty soon I went alone to her door and whispered, "Abby?" practicing the word in my head before I spoke. I said it again.

Her voice came muffled through the door. "You can still call me Ab'lene," she said. "That's totally different."

I said, "Okay." Ab'lene's what I'd called her since I could first talk. I stared at her door, hoping both that she'd open it and be all right and that she wouldn't open it at all. I waited as long as I could, then whispered, "Everything's all right, Ab'lene. It's a pretty name. I mean, what if it had been Amarillo or someplace? Lubbock?"

I heard her laugh a little, and I could picture her in there, biting her red knuckles, trying not to laugh at all. I wondered where the gun was. "Good night, Sidekick," she said.

The bats were next, but they didn't last long. One evening we were getting set to go out for them—you had to wait till almost dark, of course—and Abilene came charging up the basement steps three at a time. I stepped out of her way as she started shouting, "Where are my guns?"

Mom and Dad were watching TV and when Abilene reached that door she shouted, "Where are they?"

"Abby," Mom started and I heard a whack. Though I'd never heard it before I knew right away it was the sound of a hand against a face and I backed up until both my shoulder blades were tight against the kitchen wall.

There was more shouting then, not words, just shouts, a roar finally breaking out of Dad. In a second he came through the kitchen with Abilene pinched in his arms. She thrashed like a broken-backed snake, but she didn't have a chance caught in those arms.

Mom was right behind and she stopped long enough to say, "We're taking Abby to town, Austin." She apologized then, while I studied the bright pink outline of Abilene's fingers on her cheek. Mom was out the door when she turned and said, "You tried so hard with her."

I watched from the door, Mom getting behind the wheel while Dad held Abilene down in the backseat. She shouted to me for help, but I couldn't do anything but let the screen door bang shut between us.

When I couldn't hear the car anymore I went downstairs and found the gun rack empty, the same way Abilene had. I went through Mom and Dad's closet but our guns weren't there either.

They were in the attic, not hard to find, just behind some boxes. Both guns, Abilene's and the ruined sawed-off, and the whole garbage bag of shells Abilene had reloaded. It took two trips getting them down the ladder. It was a dumb hiding spot. If Abilene hadn't blown up like she had we'd be out right now, doing nothing more dangerous than pumping the night full of holes. Maybe a few bats too, at worst.

My parents had a long talk with me that first night. *Bipolar,* they kept saying, like Abilene was some kind of magnet. They kept saying I was great for her and that I should keep trying to be her friend. Mom did most of the talking while Dad stared at his hands.

I nodded and they said we'd all have to try to do everything we could. "You know what you could start with?" I said, looking at Dad. "Don't ever tell that story again, about the names. How All This Started."

Actually Dad hadn't told that story in a long, long time and he looked startled. I said, "We hate that."

I got up then, thinking of the two of them that first of all nights in Abilene. I couldn't keep from shaking my head, rolling my eyes. "I moved the guns," I said. "She would've found them there in a second."

Abilene didn't come home for almost two weeks. Then she was quiet for a long time, not shouting or yelling at anyone. She never asked about the guns and we never went out in her truck anymore. Sometimes I'd ask if she'd just like to go for a ride but she'd breathe slow and say, "I don't think so, Austin. Too hot."

I kept working at her though, being her friend, and when a norther came through, chilling everything, I said, "Not too hot now, Ab'lene," till she finally said she'd come along. But she made me drive, saying she wasn't quite up to that. I wasn't old enough for a license yet, but Abilene had taught me how to drive years ago.

Even though Mom and Dad were up in town, one of the first times they'd left Abilene alone with me, I waited until we were out of sight of the house before goosing it and blowing off the road. Instantly we had a red Texas roostertail climbing the sky behind us. I pointed with my thumb and when Abilene looked back I shouted, "No moss growing on our backs!"

Abilene laughed at that, laughed a long time and I slowed down just so I could hear. I was barely creeping along by the time she got over it. She wiped at her eyes and before I knew it she jerked her foot around the stick and hammered my foot down on the gas. I had a wild time just trying to steer.

When I lost it at last, ricocheting off the edge of the wash, grinding up the side of the truck, and blowing a tire clean off its bead, Abilene finally let off the gas and we lurched to a stop in the center of the wash. It was a long time before we got our breaths back enough to talk.

"Ab'lene?" I said and she answered back, "Austin?" teasing the way my voice shook.

We broke out laughing all over again until she stuck her hand under my nose. It was full of pills. "Want some?" she said. "What to know how a voodoo zombie feels?"

I shook my head and she threw all the pills out her window. She'd been skipping them for a long time, she told me. She was biding her time. "Until the perfect getaway opportunity presents itself.

"First," she said, "I was going to wait until you were old enough to come along." She punched my shoulder. "I mean, what good's an outlaw without a sidekick?"

"Outlaw?" I said.

"But can't wait that long, Sidekick," she said. "I'd never make it."

She punched my shoulder again and it hurt. She said, "But I'll be back for you. Count on that. I won't forget Austin."

"Where are you going?" I asked, but she didn't answer.

It was closing on dusk by the time we got the tire changed and the truck going again and I didn't want Abilene to go away. I drove slow up the draw and said, "Want to get a few bats?"

She stared at me a second and then smiled. "Austin, Austin," she said. She looked straight ahead and crooked her finger like pulling a trigger. "Pow."

When I showed her where the guns were, safe in the old water tank, she shook her head and said, "Austin," again, smiling so wide it seemed her face might tear. She rubbed my head the way she had when I'd hurt it bouncing into the top of the truck.

"Let's get us some bats," she said, though I would have stayed inside that old tank with her forever right then.

"Maybe swallows would be better," I said. "You can at least eat swallows."

"Nope. Bats. It's too late for swallows."

When we left with the guns, Abilene drove.

We were out late and Mom and Dad looked more at me than Abilene when we came home. "Did you two have a good time?" they asked together, Dad, even with all his size, having the same nervous bird-look as Mom. Before I could answer Abilene said, "Yes. Austin took me for a ride. It was pretty. The sun set."

How she lapsed back to her new quiet was startling. At sunset we'd been overlooking the river, blazing away at the shadowy traces of bats. I don't know if we hit any or not. We stayed out till after it was completely dark and Abilene kept shooting straight up into the night. "Look at the flame, Austin," she said every time she shot.

"I'm looking," I answered.

In the middle of that night I woke up scared, peering into the pitch black of my room, breathing hard, wondering what had woken me. I could hear the soft breathing of someone else in my room, someone standing close. Sweat popped out all over me. Then, quietly, out of the darkness, Abilene said, "You know, the only good part of the goddamn How All This Started story is the night in Austin."

"Ab'lene?" I said, and I listened to the floor creak beneath her as she walked out of my room and the gentle way she had closing the door, even turning the handle so the latch wouldn't bump over the catch.

In the morning Mom was shaking me, telling me I had to get up, I had to help. Abilene was gone, with her truck. I dressed as fast as I could, though I knew there was nothing I could do now about anything. "She doesn't have a spare tire," I said, then shook my head when Mom asked, "What?"

Mom and Dad called Abilene's doctor. My job, they told me, was to stay home. "In case she calls," Dad said.

I said, "Okay," though I knew there wasn't going to be any call. I said "Good luck" to them anyway, and they raced off on their search.

Once their dust settled I set off walking, dodging through the cactus and creosote. At the water tank the sawed-off and the bag of shells were gone, but Abilene had left me her gun and a few handfuls of shells. I worked the pump and a live shell fell out. There were five of them, a full magazine. Last night, when we put them away, the guns hadn't been loaded.

I pictured Abilene loading up the sawed-off, dropping it onto the truck seat along with the bag of shells, then coming back into the black inside of the tank and working to slide these shells into the magazine, thinking about me, not stranding me helpless.

Loading my pockets with the shells she left, I put the gun over my shoulder and stepped out of the tank, picturing Abilene thinking of me, while Mom and Dad and the doctors and who knows who all else were already chasing after her.

I walked back into the desert carrying her gun while she

drove wherever she was going with the one we'd ruined. I pictured her white-knuckled grip on the wheel, just barely keeping from knocking herself out on the roof of the cab as she launched through the ditches; the red tornado that'd follow her everywhere. No matter how far anyone chased her.

I knew Abilene was gone for good. There was no way, otherwise, that she'd ever admit there was a single good thing about How All This Started. Even me.

I walked all day, getting dirtier and sweatier and thirstier every step. I went every place we'd ever gone, every place I could reach. And when at dark I lifted Abilene's shotgun and fired into the night, the gun slapped back against me and I worked the pump quick and hard the way she does, and I fired as fast as I could, straight into the darkness. It wasn't until I was out of shells, fumbling in my pockets to reload, my ears whining with the shock of sound, that I realized I was crying. I thunked in the next five shells and fired again, fast, watching the flame.

When I was out of shells, my shoulder and ears throbbing, eyes burning, I started home, wondering if I'd make it through the darkness and the cactus, the snakes and the scorpions; everything out here Abilene had left me with.

The TV was off, but Mom and Dad were home anyway. They popped up off the couch like jack-in-the-boxes when I walked inside. I hadn't bothered wiping the tears and dirt off my face, and they looked just as tired as me.

They started to shake their heads, letting me know they hadn't found Abilene, which, of course, I knew already, but when they could really make me out in the dark doorway, still holding Abilene's gun, they stopped short. Dad sat back down hard, staring at the gun, then at my face, looking just as confused as he did that time Abilene told him to get out of our way. I set the gun down, leaning it against the wall, knowing there was nothing left for me to shoot.

Mom whispered, "Come here, Austin," and eased down beside Dad, light as a bird. She sat close, her leg touching his, and they each put an arm around each other. For the first time they didn't look ridiculous together, didn't look the way Abilene always made them look, and I could almost picture them those nights Dad used to love to tell about, amazed at his good fortune.

Night Swimming

They found my mother naked in the snow. In June. She'd escaped the nursing home a week before, and I pictured her frozen solid there by the ice of the creek. Gray, I guessed, rather than blue. She wore just one red sock.

I knew I'd never know how she got that far up into the mountains, but I couldn't stop wondering what she thought she was doing, where in her life she thought she was. After all the weariness of widowhood, raising the two of us alone, I envisioned her in the middle of something fabulously fun and daring. A midnight rendezvous at the river maybe. Skinny-dipping. Taking her clothes off in front of some boy for the very first time. A skinny guy, with a big, gap-toothed grin, just as nervous as her, his body still smooth and white, all but hairless. Somebody who'd chase her into the river, splashing and laughing, hoping to get his hands on her before she slipped away. Somebody totally different than Jenny had described Dad; the dark, distant little man in the pictures.

When Jenny would visit, we'd stand beside Mom's bed in the nursing home as Mom talked on and on about people we'd never heard of. I'd pick at my nails, trying to imagine where she was, who she was with. Jenny would act interested, humming questions, whispering, "Really!" the whole time fussing over her, slipping her old jangling bracelets around her purpling wrists, tying her hair back with her favorite scarlet ribbons; hair so white it was almost clear.

Then, at night, while I cleaned the silent halls, I'd slip into Mom's room and catch her staring at the bracelets as if she might weep. I'd sit beside her and ask what was wrong, but for once she'd be quiet, her mumbling lips still, and I'd ease down beside her, slip an arm behind her head, around her shoulders. She'd held me like that when I was just a kid, awake in the middle of the night, scared and crying but unable to answer any of her questions about what was wrong, what was scaring me. She'd whispered stories to me then, so, sliding the bracelets off her narrow wrists, hiding them away, I began telling Mom my stories, things from my life, secretly hoping it might help her remember her own.

Once—I must have been tiny, she had me so completely wrapped in her arms—she told me about swimming at night, diving down into the deep, black water, how cold and silent it was. "Deliciously silent," I remember her saying.

"When I was way, way down, deep in that blackness," she said, "something touched me! Something that moved!" Her voice and her breath came faster and she squeezed me tight. "I kicked and kicked, sucking in water, splashing to get back to the top, to get away!" My own breath was held by then, but Mom laughed softly and said, "It was so silly. It was only the boy I was swimming with. We'd bumped into each other." She stroked my forehead. "That's how it is when you're frightened, Joey. It's just something you haven't understood right."

I remember for years asking her to tell the night-swimming story again, but she'd only smile and shake her head, saving it for herself.

At the cemetery it's just a little group from the nursing home, us, and the wind. Jenny is stiff in tailored black, and I stand beside her in a borrowed navy blue jacket, which Jenny'd told me looked nice with the gray at my temples, like I could be some kind of professor.

At the nursing home I always just wore my work clothes, the gray coveralls with my name above the pocket. JOE, all in capitals. Jenny, having the three-plus interstate hours across the Idaho desert, treated the visits more like occasions and was always a little spruced up. But what was the point, I figured, with as little as Mom could tell. She once introduced us to each other as Edward and Natasha.

Edward's the guy I picture Mom skinny-dipping with before the exotic Natasha stole him away, leaving Mom behind to settle for Dad. After Edward's wild ways, the stodginess Jenny described as Dad's might even have seemed safe. Maybe not for long, but long enough to set that course for her life. Till her mind could collapse, letting her escape back to those wild years, when she'd sneak out in the middle of the night to dive naked into the grip of that black current, no idea where anything might lead.

The priest has his last say, and Jenny and I leave our handfuls of dirt with Mom. Walking away I feel as if I'll totter, and I suddenly want to ask Jenny to come live in our old house, bring her whole family. But I have to take a few deep breaths before asking only, "Will you come over for coffee?"

I'm surprised when she agrees, and grateful, but also

embarrassed to have her see our old home. When she used to visit Mom, we'd meet for lunch, Jenny making fun of Pocatello's restaurants, so far from her oasis of Boise. Then we'd go straight to the nursing home. She'd be back on the road early, getting in as much of the drive as she could before dark, home in time to help Earl tuck in their kids. She never showed any interest in seeing our home again. Even when she was so close.

But now she sees it all, starting with the lawn I'd managed to chop through this morning, but it's pretty obvious anyway; the pale yellow, sun-starved shoots and the clots of cut grass spiraling around the yard in thick green rows. As kids we always had assigned jobs, helping Mom "keep our heads above water." Until I was old enough that Mom thought it was semi-safe for me to use the mower, Jenny did the yard work. Then she switched to laundry.

Inside, Jenny lets herself down on the couch, beside a stack of books I'd gathered up but then couldn't find room for on the shelves. On the floor, where most people would have a coffee table, are the boxes of stuff I'd brought home from Mom's room. Different housedresses and robes mostly, though her pictures and cards and candy tins filled most of the smaller box. I needed the coffee table somewhere else, but right now, for the life of me, I can't remember where.

It isn't like Jenny dumped all this on me, Mom and all. With the sudden bloom of Mom's mistakes—unable to find her keys one day, her house the next—me helping out just made sense. Jenny had her own family and I was still just home, barely passing at ISU, losing more interest in my anthropology courses every semester.

When I finally admitted I couldn't keep track of her myself, couldn't keep her from hurting herself, from ambling down the road in her nightgown, a flaming red scarf tied boldly around her neck, I followed her into the nursing home the only way I could. Lately I've been back at ISU, day classes in nursing, but with Mom gone I don't know if I'll bother.

Jenny leans and lifts the broken cardboard flap of a box in front of her. Mom and Dad stare at her in black and white, the train of Mom's wedding dress pooled around their feet.

Jenny flips the piece of cardboard back and forth. Mom and Dad disappear, then flash back, young and serious. Jenny sinks back into the couch and I whisper, "Did she ever say anything to you about anyone before Dad?"

Jenny smiles. It's not the first time I've asked. "Never," she says, shaking her head. "Just Dad. Then just us."

"But before us she must have—"

"She was just our mom," Jenny says. "Don't go making up some big thing for her."

"But she must have lived once," I insist, unable to think of her just scrubbing our floors, doing our laundry, fixing our meals, the whole time cleaning other people's houses to keep our heads above water. "Before Dad died she—"

"Before Dad died she was our mom, too." Jenny opens the box top again, looks in. "She didn't have this magical life you've always wanted for her, Joe. She married a man who probably should have been a bachelor, and when he died so young she was absolutely unprepared for the world. They didn't even have life insurance. She did what she had to to raise us. Isn't that enough for you? Isn't that achievement enough?"

"Did you know she used to go swimming at night?"

Jenny looks up and shakes her head, but only to warn me not to start on anything like that.

"All the bracelets," I insist, "the scarves, the fancy belts. Were they for Dad?"

Jenny admits, "Dad wouldn't have noticed if she *painted* herself crimson."

"But where did they come from then? Who were they for?"

"She had one tiny indulgence, Joe. You can't begrudge her that. She was so proud of how she looked, despite everything."

"I'm not begrudging her a thing! I want to know who she was!"

"She was our mom. Pure and simple."

It seems so little. I stare at Jenny, sitting so well dressed, the style Mom gave her. "What would you do if Earl died?" I ask. "How well prepared are you for the world?"

Jenny draws back and I jump out of my chair. "Coffee! I forgot."

I'm halfway to the kitchen, but Jenny says, "No, Joe. None for me, thanks."

I turn and say, "I'm sorry, Jenny. I never meant . . ."

She waves her hand, as if nothing I say could touch her. She pulls the wedding photo into her lap. "That dress," she says, staring into their smooth, unmarked faces. Neither of them are smiling, but maybe that was the fashion back then.

Jenny sets the picture carefully back on top of the others in the small box, then stands and walks to the staircase.

She stops at the lighter square in the darkened wallpaper where the wedding photo hung all those years. "Are you still searching for her private stash?" she asks. "Her bundles of love letters?"

It's something I'd asked her about, something Jenny insists that, even if they existed, Mom would never have left for prying eyes.

I shake my head. "No." I lie. "It was just something I wondered about." But I can't resist adding, "Wouldn't it be wonderful, if there were such a thing?"

Jenny gives a tired smile. She glances over her shoulder at the yard, the mountains still white near the peaks, the snow retreating even in the days since they found Mom. "It's time," she says.

I had thought she might stay, at least this one night. I say, "I know it looks like hell down here, but I cleaned your room for you, Jenn."

She reaches out and touches the shoulder of my borrowed jacket. "Thanks, Joe," she says. "But I'm late as it is."

"Late? You'll be home in time to fix dinner."

She gives me a look, meaning, *Well, that is my job,* and I look at her feet, her nice black shoes, the black nylons. "I thought we might have dinner someplace," I say.

"We will, Joe," she promises. "Just not tonight. Maybe you should come to Boise this weekend. There's a new Basque place everybody's talking about. It'll be my treat."

I figure she means I can go to the promised land of Boise now whenever I want, that I don't have to worry about leaving Mom anymore. Or maybe that Boise is where we'll see each other from now on, that she won't be making that deadly boring drive across the desert one more time, won't subject herself to one more backwater Pocatello restaurant.

I pick up the picture box and follow Jenny out to her car.

She says, "You should keep all of that," but she opens the trunk for me, then shuts it quick over the box. That gaping hole in the series of photos going up the stairs will be there forever now.

"What are you going to do, Joe?" Jenny finally asks.

I look away from the mountains. "Try to get some sleep, I guess." I shrug. "Go to work tonight."

"Are you going to get off night shift?"

"I'm a janitor, Jenny," I remind her. "There aren't a lot of day shifts."

She touches my shoulder again, opening her door with her other hand. "You can do whatever you want now, Joe."

"They found her up at Spirit Creek," I tell her.

Jenny flinches and instead of slipping behind the wheel, she takes a big breath. "You already told me that, Joe."

"Just sitting by the bank. Way up high, where the creek's just getting going. You can jump across it up there."

"Did you go up there, Joe?" she asks, her hand still on my shoulder. "Tell me you didn't torture yourself that way."

"Just sitting by the bank in the crusty old snow," I answer. "Sitting there with that one red sock." The whole place was trampled with footprints by the time I got there; hiker, police, coroner. I couldn't find where she'd sat down that last time.

Jenny stares and stares at me. "Why don't you come with me right now, Joe?" she asks. "Take a night off. I'll bring you back Monday in time for work."

I smile. "Wouldn't you know it'd be red," I say. "Her favorite color. Bright, blazing scarlet. Like some kind of palace guard."

"There's nothing you could have done, Joe," Jenny tells me.

"Just like her to leave that one touch, even if it was only a sock."

"Nothing, Joe," Jenny says again. "I'm telling you. Not one thing."

"I looked everywhere I ever heard her mention. Even places Edward and Natasha went. But I don't remember hearing anything about Spirit Creek. Do you?"

Jenny's biting her lip. "No, Joe," she says. "Never." Then, "Come with me. You can stay as long as you like."

I grin. Wouldn't Earl just love that? But I say thanks, then wave a hand back toward our old house and shake my head. "Look at this place, Jenny. Wouldn't believe it could get like this in just a couple of weeks, would you?" Ten days really, since she escaped. "I've got to get after it."

"It'll wait," Jenny whispers.

"Word gets out I live in a mess like this . . . Wouldn't do, Jenn. Not for a janitor. I mean, if I can't keep my own place clean . . . My career could be finished."

"It's not a career, Joe."

"I'll find something," I promise, glad I never told her about the nursing classes.

She slips behind the wheel and says, "I'll call."

"Check out that Basque place for me. See if it's worth the drive."

She promises she will, and then she's gone. I watch her go before turning back inside.

There's still one corner of the attic I haven't searched, wondering what I'd do when there was nowhere else to look, but I head upstairs, thinking I can probably get through it before the sun heats the roof, makes the insulation cling to my sweaty arms. A person couldn't really destroy every trace of their sane life, could they? They'd have to hold back something, wouldn't they, something they'd know was still there, that they could steal away and look at, remember?

The box I saved for last, the one that looked most promising, is full of clothes washed and ironed and folded for the Salvation Army. Judging by the styles, boxed and folded since the sixties sometime. There are a few outfits of Jenny's, little-girl dresses, and one baby jumper that must have been mine, but otherwise it's all Dad's, probably things she'd cleaned out of the closets after his funeral, then maybe hadn't had the heart to throw away. But, seeing the thoroughness with which she's obliterated her past, I guess it's more likely that she simply became overwhelmed raising me and Jenny, rather than growing sentimental over a box of flare-legged, neon-hued polyesters. This box must have just been shoved aside, and then put up here, out of the way. There isn't so much as a glove of my mother's in there.

Is it really possible that there simply wasn't anything for her to hide?

Jenny calls a few days later. My ear rustles against the pillow and I don't make out what she's saying, so when she pauses, I ask, "Is this about that Basque place?"

Her pause stretches out. "What?" she says. Then, "Joe, are you in bed? It's practically dinnertime." She sounds afraid of something. "Tell me you're not in bed," she says.

"I am," I answer. "I work nights. Remember?"

"Oh, Joe. I'm sorry."

"It's okay," I say. "I had to get up any second now," and right then Mom's old Big Ben alarm clock starts clanging. I hear Jenny laugh.

I slap at the clock till it quits, then sit on the edge of my narrow mattress, the bed I've slept in all my life. Rubbing my face, I say, "Okay, Jenn. What's up?"

"Well, first, how are you? How have you been holding up?"

"Got the house back on its running legs," I say. "You wouldn't recognize it if you saw it."

"You know what I mean," she says.

"She's been in another world for a decade, Jenn. This wasn't some terrible, sad thing."

She pauses again, even longer than the first time. "But, the way she, out alone like that—"

"I don't think she was alone," I say. "I don't think she thought she was."

"Joe," she says sternly, as if to snap me out of it, to break me away from the same dreamy trail Mom had taken. Like Alzheimer's is something you might catch. "Earl's been talking to a lawyer," she continues. "He says the case is foolproof. There was supposed to be security. It was their job to see she didn't wander off."

I swallow. "I wouldn't want to do anything like that," I say. I wish I had some clothes on.

"She should still be alive, Joe!"

"Alive," I repeat. I can hear Jenny breathing.

"Earl," she says, then corrects herself. "We. We've already filed suit. I was calling to tell you, so you could be part of it." She breathes again.

"You know what I think she was doing, Jenn?" I say.

"Mom?" That fear's back in her voice.

"Skinny-dipping," I say. "I can practically see it. Swimming bare-naked with Edward. Probably not in Spirit Creek, but somewhere where the water was bigger. The Snake maybe. That might have been where they met Natasha. Maybe she was naked, too. I think Edward followed Natasha away. Name like that, she'd have to be beautiful, don't you think?" If you ever told Mom she looked nice, she'd laugh and say she was nothing but bean-skinny-homely, like it was one word.

Jenny waits for me to go on, but I don't know anything more about it.

"And you say you don't think it's sad?" she says at last.

"I think she must've been pretty excited. I mean, stripping down with Edward, even if there was only moonlight. Even if they were just going swimming. Even if Natasha was lurking in the shadows."

"She should still be alive, Joe. She should still be able to go swimming with Edward every day."

"But she was getting so weak, Jenn. I'm glad she went doing something she wanted."

"We're going ahead with this, Joe," Jenny tells me. "I'll split the settlement with you, whether you join us or not."

Now I'm the one who waits before I can speak. "Those people, Jenn," I say. "At the home. They're my friends."

"No they're not, Joey," she says. She hasn't called me Joey in ages. "They're employees."

"They're my friends too, Jenn. The employees, and the people who live there. I've gotten to know them all."

"But she's gone, Joe. You've got to move on."

"I am," I assure her, though I don't have any idea where I'd go, even which direction my first step should be in.

"We won't hurt your friends, Joey," Jenny says. "The home's insurance will cover whatever happens."

I take a deep breath. "I work there, Jenn. That's where I work."

"What? You work for that office company. What's it called?"

"The home had an opening," I say. "It just made things easier. You know how her nightgowns kept disappearing? Her jewelry? This way I could keep an eye on things."

Her voice is scratchy. "When, Joe? When did you do this?"

"A while ago," I say. I pull on my socks, one after the other, pinching the phone against my shoulder.

"How long?"

"A few years now," I admit. It will be eight years next month.

She coughs or something, then nothing else.

"Are you okay?" I ask. "Jenn?"

"I'm coming over, Joe," she says. "I'll be there before nine."

"I'll be at work."

"Take the night off."

"I couldn't do that. They count on me."

"Just tonight," she pleads. "For me."

"I can't," I say. "I've never taken a day off. They'd think something bad had happened."

"Joe."

"I wouldn't want to scare them."

"I'm coming anyway."

I stop, my pants up one leg. "Your room's all ready, Jenn! You can stay here. Really, it's not as bad as you saw it. I even found the coffee table. It was in my truck. I'd taken it to the home for Mom to put her pictures on. Completely forgot about it." I give a little laugh.

Jenny doesn't say anything. Maybe she hadn't noticed the table was missing.

"I'll be really quiet coming home, Jenn," I promise. "You can sleep as late as you want."

When I get in that night, I walk around Jenny's car, petting the hood, which has long since cooled after her drive. I can't stop smiling.

I tiptoe inside and find Jenny not in her room, but on the couch, slouched against the stack of books, the one thing in the house I haven't yet found a place for. They're my textbooks, all old and out of date, but I can't make myself throw them away. Some nights I look at them, wondering about that life I'd once started. Digging for bones, I can't help but wonder. What spell was I under? When there's so much to do here and now. Before the bone stage. Before the fossils.

Sneaking up to the linen closet, I pull out the old afghan Mom always put over us when we stayed home sick, that I'd just brought back from the home. I'd hand washed it in the basement sink, thinking I was just cleaning it for storage.

Tiptoeing back into the living room, I unfold the afghan in the air, its clean smell wrapping around me. I drape it over Jenny as carefully as I used to tuck in Mom in the middle of the night, my JOE uniform starchy, my hands rough and boiled from cleaning and scrubbing and polishing.

I wrap the afghan around Jenny's legs, keeping out any drafts, then pull the fringed edge up close to her chin, turning the fringe under so it won't tickle her neck. She'll have that clean smell with her all night long that way. It's then that I notice Jenny's scarf; the filmy, silky flash of scarlet wrapped loosely around her neck, something a movie star would wear, or Mom. I'd put it in with the pictures I packed for Jenny, and I smile, knowing she'd gone through those things.

The sun's not long in coming, and when the room first lightens, I'm still in the rocker right across from Jenny, my feet up on the edge of the coffee table.

The scarf's all but covered by the afghan, so I lean forward, almost out of my chair, and tug the afghan down a touch, just enough to catch the full, bold effect.

But something I do, tugging at the afghan, the creak of the rocker, maybe only the sun coming through the undrawn curtains, wakes Jenny. Her eyes pop open, looking directly into mine.

"Good morning," I whisper.

Jenny reaches for me, but her hand snarls in the bright knots of the afghan. "Joey," she says.

She looks frightened, like she might not be sure where she's woken. I murmur, "Everything's all right," and she gives a tiny, uncertain nod.

"I used to sit with Mom like this during my breaks," I tell Jenny. "Even sometimes when I should've been working. She went through a phase where she could hardly sleep two hours in a row. Did I tell you about that?"

Jenny watches me, shakes her head.

"She seemed to like it," I say, "finding me with her. It seemed to comfort her.

"If she was quiet, I told her stories. I told her how sitting with her like this reminded me of when I was a boy. How she once told me about swimming at night with Edward."

I straighten the afghan over Jenny's legs.

"Joey," Jenny says, slipping her fingers out of the afghan's knots and taking my hand in hers. "There was no Edward."

"You know," I answer, "I think maybe you're right. I kept looking for him, for some trace, but I think now that maybe Edward wasn't in her past. All those years, though, keeping herself sharp, that special touch was still for him. She was *waiting* for him, Jenn."

"Joey, you've got to stop."

"He's come for her, Jenny. That's all. There's nothing to be afraid of. Or sad about. He's just finally come."

The Investigator

The table was set, steam rising from the first bowl Victor's wife placed on the lace cloth. There was a new centerpiece, some live plant, a cyclamen Victor guessed, with blooms like explosions. She was trying to make an occasion of this and Victor tried not to let her see how that irritated him. He stared at the cratered surface of the steaming potatoes and listened to the rain pelting the wavery old glass of the dining room windows. She was humming slightly, abstractedly, and Victor couldn't help but hear it. The phone began to ring and instead of listening to her answer he looked out at the night and the rain.

The dark, cold drizzle was fitting, Victor thought—not wildly bursting flowers and cheerful whistling. After all, Jerome was not coming home from Stockholm with a Nobel prize under his arm. He was coming home from Cornell after only one semester, weighed down with nothing more than his luggage. He could still go back, Ginny kept reminding him. He just hadn't been ready.

Victor crushed his napkin in his lap. Things like failure, like quitting, didn't simply vanish. Though walking away might seem simple at the time, Victor knew it would mark Jerome like a stain for the rest of his life.

Youthful exuberance they'd called it. A shame they'd said. Maybe it was the same shame and exuberance that kept him so late, with Ginny out there fixing his lamb roast, pretending he would be here any minute, that nothing was wrong.

"It's for you," Ginny whispered.

Victor turned away from the dark, rain-splotched windows and looked at her standing in the doorway.

"It's work," she said. And she gave him a look telling him to put it off, telling him not to leave her now, not to leave him.

"I thought it might have been Jerome," Victor said. "Deigning to reveal his whereabouts."

"He'll be along. He was probably expecting to be picked up."

"Yes. I wouldn't doubt that," Victor said, but they'd been over that before. He pushed his chair across the glossy parquet and placed his rumpled, unused napkin on the tablecloth. Victor pictured his son standing in the rain outside the train station, pacing back and forth, maybe just slumped against a railing, waiting, like a child, for his parents to come and make everything all right.

He stepped away from the table, saying, "I'll take it in the den."

The streetlights lit the den sufficiently and Victor did not bother with the light switch. He rather liked the gloom. When he picked up the phone, he listened for the kitchen extension being replaced on the hook. Only then did he say hello, and as he talked he studied the walnut top of his desk, nearly black in the dusky room, with even darker runnels shifting across its surface. He glanced once at the rain-streaked window, the source of the shadows coursing across the polished surface of his desk, then looked back to the shadows. The patterns were jagged, like lightning drawn by children, but the edges were blurred by the distance between the window and desk. He thought of lightning caught just at the edge of one's vision—indistinct and perhaps even fooling one into doubting its existence, but crackling hot and searing the air with its thunder soon enough.

He was just finishing his conversation when he heard the front door snap shut and Ginny's happy chatter. As he stepped from the den he heard his son's voice. "I had to take a cab." It sounded like a simple explanation, not a petulant accusation, and Victor buttoned the center button of his suit jacket and walked toward the front hall.

They stood there, his wife and son, interrupted in their embrace, breaking apart awkwardly when Victor stepped into the hallway. The lighting here was just as feeble as it had been in the den—depending on outside light and the indirect glow of distant illuminated rooms. Victor saw his son straighten and turn to face him head-on. A cornered animal preparing for a charge or a boy trying to make an impression—Victor was not sure which.

Victor stepped to the doorway and slapped at the panel of light switches. The porch went dark, but the hall flashed in white light, even the light at the top of the stairway coming on. The glare was stunning, but Victor said, "For heaven's sake, you'd think we lived in a tomb."

He glanced at his son, not at his face, but more at the space he filled again in the house. "Your mother's fixed lamb. The way you like it." He held his hand out for his son's coat. "It's all ready. Get to it."

Instead of surrendering his coat, Jerome took Victor's outstretched hand and shook it. Victor almost stepped backward—nearly withdrew his hand as if some punishment were due. But he stopped, only barely flinching, and he shook Jerome's hand. He looked then at the face, capped with the same shock of unruly black hair as his own, lidded with the same band of heavy, even bushy, black eyebrows. Below them his own eyes looked back, black and burning, with an intensity he had once considered so promising. He broke off the handshake and turned for the dining room. "Come, come," he said, "it's all getting cold."

Victor stood at the head of the table, readying himself for his announcement as he listened to Jerome hang up his coat. Ginny and Jerome came into the room together and she pulled out his chair for him. Jerome said thank you, then something about all the trouble being unnecessary. She pooh-poohed that and started for the kitchen, smiling hopefully at Victor and telling him to sit down, she'd take care of everything.

Victor remained standing, hands on the back of his chair. He surveyed the table and noticed that a cover had been put over the potatoes she'd left so hopefully open. A wisp of steam still escaped through a small notch in the lid's edge. The notch was meant for a spoon, Victor thought, for a spoon to be inserted and then still covered if things did not go according to plan—everything kept that ready.

Ginny came in with the leg of lamb and set the platter in front of Victor's place. "Sit, sit," she said, so near to bursting.

"I have to leave," Victor said.

"Victor!" Ginny clapped her hands together and then held them, as if in prayer. Jerome looked down at his empty plate.

"That was Thomas on the phone. It's the San Diego collision."

"I don't care what it is. There are certain priorities that have to be made." Ginny's voice shook the smallest bit.

"This has been prioritized. Fingers are pointing at the traffic controllers. The black boxes just arrived on a charter."

"Let someone else do it."

"It is my responsibility."

"There are other things that you are responsible for."

"One hundred and thirty-seven people were killed," Victor said. "Our son merely dropped out of school."

That made both of them look away from Victor, as if he were the one who'd made such a hash of things. He sighed and let go of his chair. "Ginny, this has nothing to do with anything else. Honestly. There is nothing I would rather do than sit and eat as a family. But, at this moment, I cannot."

Victor pulled his chair out and offered it to Jerome. "Would you take my place and carve for your mother?"

Jerome stood up, long and lanky, fully grown. "When will you be back?" he asked, still without looking at Victor.

"I don't know. This shouldn't run too late. I'm sure I'll be leaving for San Diego though. Tomorrow or Wednesday."

His son eased into his chair and nodded. He picked up the long, thin carving knife and held it without beginning to cut anything. Ginny stared at Victor until he went to the front hall and took his overcoat from the closet. He was tightening the belt when he heard them begin to speak at the table. He was glad for that, glad for Ginny. When he opened the front door he heard Jerome call, "We'll save some for you."

Victor paused, then placed his hat on his head and stepped into the rain.

He drove slowly toward the capitol area and the FAA building. Rain was everywhere, although it no longer fell from the sky. Each streetlight made white, watery circles on the pavement and round rainbows in the black air.

When the call first came in, Victor had leapt at the opportunity to escape his house. He was ashamed of that. More than a hundred people really had died, and it was his son, after all, who was coming home. He heard Jerome's voice again, wearily explaining that he'd had to take a cab, almost apologizing for his tardiness in the same few words. Victor noticed the scent of the cooking lamb still on his clothes and he bent forward slightly to smell it more clearly.

When he reached the offices he parked in the underground lot. The dry pavement rang under his feet, echoing away in the empty spaces. He stood quietly in the elevator, holding his briefcase before him like a shield. He'd grown to dread these black-box sessions—the eavesdropping on the last minutes of so many lives—and he realized that if Jerome had not been coming home he would have tried to escape this any way he could.

The elevator whooshed open and the others were there, waiting for him. "They're just about ready," Thomas told him. Victor took up a seat, sweating, he realized, though the room was chilly with air conditioning.

They had some trouble with the tape, and at one point the playback machine quit. They were still in the routine part— the big airliner circling in a holding pattern—and people around the table were drinking coffee and smoking cigarettes. While the tape played Victor began picturing the cockpit crew, impatient and bored, flying in circles so close to home. The flight engineer made a small joke about the head stewardess, who must have been getting on in both years and weight, and the pilots laughed, the tedium evident in every strained chuckle. Some people around the table smiled nervously.

They would confer when they reached the end of the

tape—the point of final impact. The private plane that struck the 727 had no recorder they could listen to. Victor looked at his watch. It was much later than he had guessed, and he wondered if Ginny and Jerome had gone to bed yet, or if they were up late, talking as they had in the past.

The conference lasted until well past midnight. The rain had started again sometime during the long talks, and Victor drove back through the fresh drizzle. At a deserted red light he watched the reflection of the warning color on the glistening pavement. On the crossroad the green shining changed to yellow and then red. A moment later his light turned green, but Victor sat behind the wheel and rubbed at his eyes, burning with the cigarette smoke and the hour. The wipers slapped and squeaked through the thin rain. He sat through the entire sequence of lights before continuing home.

His house was dark and he parked carefully in the garage, the automatic door groaning shut as he turned the key in the side entrance of his home. He walked through his shadowed house with quiet, practiced assurance. His den was open and he placed his briefcase just inside the door. It contained transcripts of the voice recorder and he did not want to look at them now.

The lights outside still filtered through the window, gray and watery, spilling across his desk. Victor glanced around the shadowed bookcases and the vaguely wild silhouette of Ginny's plants against the flat light of the glass. A single red eye glowed for an instant from behind his desk and Victor's heart missed a beat.

"Dad?" Jerome asked. "Is that you?"

Victor flinched again. Ginny would have said someone had walked over his grave. Anger slipped in behind the fright, and he was vastly irritated that Jerome would foul his den with a cigarette. "Smoking now?" he snapped.

The small red glow went out. "Oh, sorry," Jerome said, again sounding only as if he meant it.

Victor stood in the door, picturing Jerome smiling, pinching out the glowing hot coal between his young fingers, a frat trick, all he'd learned at college. He forced himself into the room and sat in one of the leather chairs facing the desk. He felt ridiculously as if he were being interviewed by an unknown being. He wished he'd turned on the lights.

"How'd it go?" Jerome asked.

"Pardon me?" Victor said.

"The investigation. The black box."

"Oh. Same as ever."

"What's that like? Listening to that?"

"It's just work."

There was a silence before Jerome said, "So, this is where you work."

"I do some of my work here," Victor said, but this was absurd. Jerome knew all this. "Some at the office."

"Are you going to San Diego?"

"Yes." Jerome was a flat black outline against the water channeling down the long, old windows. The water looked less like lightning now. In the pale light of the street it looked more like an enormous, writhing spiderweb, his son trapped at its center.

"I read about the crash," Jerome said. "Before I left."

Still Victor said nothing.

"I saw the pictures," Jerome said. "Wreckage everywhere. Everything all burned up. I thought, Dad'll be going there."

Jerome shifted, the leather of the chair rustling under his thin legs. "Do you mind if I smoke?"

"I'd rather you didn't," Victor said. "Not in here."

Victor heard the crinkling of the thin cellophane stop abruptly. Jerome said, "Oh, right."

Victor pounced on the hard line in his son's voice, the one he'd waited for all night. "So," he said, " 'how'd it go' for you?"

"About like you'd think," Jerome answered.

But Victor didn't want an answer. "I don't think about it," he said.

"Just too much fun, Dad. That's all."

"Fun?" Victor shot back.

There was another silence and Victor could hear his son suck in air, almost as if he was pulling on an imaginary cigarette. Maybe he had one he hadn't lit.

"Yeah, Dad. Fun," Jerome said. "Do you remember having fun? Ever?"

"What?" Victor blurted, then before Jerome could answer, he went on. "Just imagine, Jerome, just imagine how much *fun* it's been telling everyone our son had to quit Cornell after one semester. One!"

"This has been awful tough on you, Dad. Hasn't it?"

Jerome stressed the "you" and Victor heard all the self-pity he'd expected to hear when his son had explained about the taxi. " 'Oh, Jerome?' " Victor said, almost shouting. " 'Academic suspension, actually. Thrown out of the dormitory. He'll be living with us a while longer. He's thinking about a career at Burger King. Assistant manager is not beyond the possible. The sky's the limit for that boy!' "

For an instant, watching his son's silhouette caught in its web, Victor listened to his own voice. He pictured a room full of people seated around a large, heavy table, drinking coffee from Styrofoam cups and smoking cigarettes, listening to the tape of this conversation. They carved patterns in their cups with their thumbnails, smiling awkwardly now and then, heads ducked in embarrassment for the recorded voices. Victor took a deep breath and rubbed his hands against his face.

Jerome laughed a little, not happily. "You know, I stayed up just to talk to you. Can you believe that?"

Victor couldn't think of any way to answer.

"I left the light off, thinking that'd help. Like maybe we could forget it was each other we were talking to. So maybe we could talk like normal people."

Victor didn't say anything. He pictured the people around that table, leaning forward, waiting for his answer, hoping for the key to unravel the entire disaster.

"When are you going to San Diego?" Jerome asked.

"Tomorrow."

The leather under his son rustled again. Jerome stood up and walked to the window, facing away from his father. "Do you remember that we used to have fun, Dad?"

Victor watched him, and Jerome went on. "I remember once on the boardwalk, on the roller coaster, going so high I thought I'd cry. But you were right there next to me, and you were laughing and laughing. You said, 'We fall now, there won't be any survivors.' "

Jerome laughed that way again. "Once my roommate and I got talking about our earliest memories and I told him that." Jerome turned to face the room, but Victor knew his son would be unable to see him after looking out at the lights. "He was jealous," Jerome said. "Jealous. Of you. Of us."

Victor walked to the windows, looking past the tiny streams clinging to the glass. "The pilots of that plane never saw it coming," he said quietly. "They were doing everything right. They'd been in a holding pattern for an hour. You could hear how bored they were. Then the Cessna came in."

Victor traced one of the thin streams with his finger, the glass surprisingly cold. "You know what they said? Oh, for a second there was a rush of commands and questions and procedure. But after that? After they knew it was done?"

"No. I don't know what they said."

"There was a pause, a silence for a second, then the pilot just said, 'Looks like we're going in.' Then, after another second, the copilot said, 'Yep.'" Victor turned away from the window but he could not find his son or anything else in the darkness. "That was it."

"What'll you find? In San Diego?"

"Wreckage," Victor said. He looked toward the sound of his son's voice, but could not see him. "It'll be pilot error probably. On the Cessna's part. Maybe controllers, but it doesn't look like that now."

"I've got a month before the next semester starts," Jerome said.

Victor heard the question in his son's voice. "You wouldn't want to go," he answered before thinking. "Not for this."

"I don't know," Jerome said. "Maybe I would. I think I should know more about what you do."

"What I do?" Victor said, turning back to the glass and the lights. "What I do is eavesdrop, Jerome. I listen to things people never meant for me or anyone to hear again. Things that suddenly become their last words on this earth."

"What do you think they'd say if they knew?"

Victor stood tracing the path of the cold water again, blinded by the brightness of the lights outside, but able to feel Jerome close beside him. "That's the question," he said. "What I've always wondered." He paused. "I don't have any idea. There'd be so much to say I doubt, if they knew, that they'd be able to get a word out."

"What would you say?" Jerome whispered. "How would you answer, 'Looks like we're going in'?"

Victor was silent for a moment, tapping his finger against the glass, as if trying to get the light's attention. "In the last second? With nothing left but the ground?" Victor left pauses between his questions but Jerome wouldn't help.

Victor reached an arm out to his son but touched only emptiness. He chuckled suddenly, nervously—he was so sure he had felt him standing beside him.

He turned to the room, but was as blinded as Jerome must have been when he had turned that way. "I don't understand why we insist on standing in this darkness."

"Dad!" Jerome pressed. "What would you say?"

Victor looked for him in the darkness. "If I knew? If I were given that chance?"

His son stood near, but invisible, silent.

"I guess I'd say, 'Forgive me, Jerome.' I'd have to."

The Raw Material of Ash

When they burn you these days, they don't leave much behind. Not much to hand over to the grieving spouse after all those years, a whole life. Just a smudge of ash. Maybe in the old days you'd get a box of gritty meal, some rattly flakes and chips of leftover bone. But with the furnaces they have now, the high-tech torching, you'd be lucky to retrieve the smudge. What do they say we are, 70 percent water? Not a lot of ash in that.

Even so, if ash was all I had left of Denise, I'd hold on to it as if it were my own life. Tell the truth, it pretty much would be my life. Even now, young as we are.

These boxes I bang together—what they burn them in— are called cremation caskets. But there's no bronze or walnut here, no silky lining or plush padding. Nothing but reject plywood and a few sticks of one-by-one. A little glue and a handful of staples. Some Sheetrock screws.

It's all piecework to me, and since I worked up a system I

can fill the order in just over five hours. Not quite fifteen minutes per. Last bit of craftsmanship to ever touch the deceased. But I hurry to get home to Denise, see if there's something I might still do among the living.

The first time I came home early, after I'd filled enough orders to really get humming, Denise only asked, "What?" Maybe she meant what happened to the footing wall I'd thought I'd be forming, scratching around in the freezing spring mud, but probably something more like, *What are you doing here in the middle of the day? What now? What next?*

But I managed a grin, standing in the mudroom door, wriggling out of my coveralls. "Got a casket order," I told her. "Inside all day."

She acted like she actually heard what I said. "A what?" she asked, really looking at me. "Caskets?"

It was a fair question. When we first got married, that rushed summer right after high school, we talked about all the houses I'd build; how it was really something, making something with my own hands, places people would love, would live in, would have babies in; all things we were already planning on ourselves. So, when I started banging scrap plywood into boxes to burn people in, I didn't run right home and brag it up to Denise.

Finally out of my coveralls, I stepped into our house and watched Denise sitting there waiting for an explanation. Even now I can still feel surprised that she actually married me.

Of course, back then, people guessed they knew why. And standing before the J.P., the whole thing *did* feel like a trick I'd pulled on Denise. The second she'd told me she was pregnant, I'd blurted, "Let's get married!" At first she laughed, but then she got wound up, like it'd be a great joke; her with everything, marrying me with nothing. She was eighteen and she liked the idea of shocking all those people.

But after the weekend honeymoon, Denise lost her nerve. Every night I'd come home and she'd tell me again how we were just kids, we weren't parents yet, weren't ready for that. She'd say we had to hurry, that pretty soon it would be too late and we'd be trapped into the rest of our lives. I'd try to say how that's what I wanted, that we had to start somewhere, but she trailed me around the two rooms of our tiny apartment, begging. When I finally gave in—spent that terrible morning at the clinic—she came out white, but managed a smile, saying we'd sure confuse all those people who thought they knew everything. I'd tried to smile back, but what I wanted was gone.

Within a few weeks she asked her parents for the money to get our own house started—the lot, the materials. She always said she'd never ask her parents for anything, no matter what. I told her we had to give it back, but Denise answered, "I can't stay in this apartment."

"Denise. We're just starting. It's going to take some time."

"You can't want me to stay here," she said.

We built our whole house together, Denise a whirlwind once again. I'd come home at night amazed at how much she'd gotten done alone. Somehow I found time to make some furniture, and we pictured the whole trade like an art. "You're talented," Denise kept telling me. Naturally, at eighteen, I couldn't start right out on my own, so I kept on with Buckfinch—just till we got our feet under us, when Denise promised we could try again for a baby. Twelve years later, I'm still with Buckfinch. I haven't put together so much as a footstool in years. Things just happened that way. I can't quite say how.

I looked around Denise at our immaculate house, realizing that's the only way I had to explain any of this. Things just happened this way.

Denise kept waiting for an answer. "Did you say caskets?" she asked again.

"More like boxes," I said, wanting to walk back out into the garage. "For cremating people in."

"What in the world?"

"Forest Acres orders a couple dozen now and then," I explained. I tried a smile. "The people must drop off like doughnuts."

"Since when have you been doing that?" she asked, like she's adding it to some checklist—how long she's been keeping house with some scab wood butcher, wondering where her custom-home builder had vanished. Hell, some days I wonder the same thing.

"Bucky has me do them," I said. She knows I'm as close to a finish carpenter as Bucky will ever get. "They're just raw material for ash, but they got to look like you at least tried."

"And they bury people in them? The things you make?"

"Burn them," I corrected. "I'm not making anything for posterity," I admitted. "Even under ground."

She kept staring at me, dropping her mouth open as if to say, *Would you just listen to yourself?*

"Anyway," I said, glancing around the kitchen. This was as close to a conversation as we'd had in ages. I tried to think of any of the plans I'd made for things we could do if I ever got off early, if I ever surprised Denise at home before she could make up an excuse to be someplace else, someplace without me. "I got an afternoon free," I started.

"Myra's picking me up," she broke in, without waiting to see what I might've had in mind. "She's late already."

Denise got up and walked over to the window, peeking out, like Myra might have been waiting out there all along.

I walked up behind her at the window and thought of how once I would've put a hand on each side of her hips, pressed up against her, pulling her tight, just waiting for the time she'd whisper something about another baby.

But I imagined her spinning away, her move grown slick and smooth as any running back's, muttering something like *If you knew you were going to take the day off, maybe you should've called*, when all that would have done is gotten her out of the house before I saw her.

So, instead of touching her, I finally just said, "What are you and Myra doing that's so important?"

"Nothing near as vital as making boxes to burn people in," she answered right back.

And then there was Myra's impatient honk, like they're still in high school or something.

I said, "Denise," but she headed for the door. I called her name again louder, "Denise!" like she was just having trouble hearing me is all.

Half the time I don't even know if it's Myra she's out with. There's people we went to school with who are doctors now, lawyers, way out there ahead of us for everybody to see. Especially Denise.

I bang out the next order in record time, wondering about Denise; what she does all day, hell, just what she thinks about anymore. I tear through the saw work first, lucky to have any fingers left after ripping the ply, crosscutting it to length, banging out the sticks. I start thinking I'll rush through this and sneak home, see if there's something we might do again, both of us.

I slam the router through its paces, filling the air with splinters as much as shavings. Ninety-six handholds just big enough for four fingers, the quick lift into the incinerator.

Then, pieces stacked everywhere—sides, tops, bottoms—I grab the stapler and glue jug and let the dust fly. Slap the box together and screw down the lid. They'll have to get that off again. Once.

They need a box to burn them in like they need a hole in the head. What's the point? Slide the poor departed on the belt, open the doors, poof, same results.

But it's the ash, you see? What they hand over to you in that little cardboard carton, or one of those spendy urns if you've got the cash and the inclination, isn't your poor old spouse of fifty years. It's maybe one one-hundredth that person you gave your life to. The rest is just my junk plywood, sticks and glue.

The boxes are worse than any I've ever made; all out of square, edges overhanging corners, everything chipped and frayed. I try not to look at them as I load them into the truck. Bucky wanted me to deliver this batch myself, even drawing a map showing how to stack a full dozen in at once. Only way to keep it to two trips.

I'm halfway home, planning on surprising Denise into really doing something with me for the afternoon, anything, before I realize this delivery is going to eat up half the day and I'm not making a dime more for it. Bucky and his goddamn map.

I swing by the house anyway, figuring I can still ask Denise out for lunch. Even if the truck is full of caskets. Maybe it'll be something she'll decide to like. Trying to plan a joke for her, something to let her have fun again, I suddenly remember ages ago, in high school, how Denise and I used to park out by the graveyard to make out. She used to say the way we went at it we might wake the dead, find ourselves surrounded by stiffs. All of a sudden I'm driving around with this big, dumb grin, remembering how she even used to call it a stiffy, in their honor. But it was in the graveyard that she got pregnant, and I know she wouldn't think anything about that was funny.

Denise isn't home. I walk through all the rooms, each one emptier than the last. "Come on, Denise," I whisper into the stillness of my own house.

She's got the place as clean as ever, frigging sanitized, which suddenly makes me feel like we're living in a motel, like there's no real people here, nobody who will stay long, spend too much time talking over the morning coffee and have to rush out to their days, leaving their cups at their places, their chairs pushed back every which way from the table.

I pull out one of the chairs and sit down. The table is smoked glass, gleaming, and I sit back far enough I won't see my reflection. After the morning straightening-up, she's got a whole day left to fill. I glance along the fir baseboards, clear vertical grain every inch of it, which, when we built this place, Denise polyurethaned while I was at work, miles more than I could ever nail down each night. I had no idea our home could be a place this hollow, almost echoey, like a just-finished house, waiting for the first owners to make it their own.

I press my fingerprints onto the glass tabletop, whole rows of them, remembering how Denise used to jump into my arms at the end of the day, not even waiting inside half the time, but meeting me right out in the driveway, how proud it used to make me feel, that someone like her could be so excited to see me.

Eventually, leaving my fingerprints smudged all over the table like some kind of animal tracks, I go back outside and sit in the truck, the caskets stacked and tied all over behind me. I rub at my face, my throat gone dry and tight, like I've been stood up for a date—a trip to a crematorium.

Finally I back out fast, the plywood creaking and shifting enough I keep myself from screeching away.

Myra's car is out front of her house and I honk, getting a little grin out of that. She comes out in her robe, middle of the lunch hour. I yell, "Denise here?" already knowing the answer.

She shakes her head, but I don't miss the quick bite she gives her lip, the glance this way and that, her not-too-quick brain working on something quick to say. She comes up with, "Haven't seen her."

If Denise is up to something, I think, she could sure use some better allies than this. I drive off without saying another word.

I wind up running through McDonald's. Get Big Mac lettuce all over my lap by the time I pull up at Forest Acres. Brush off as I walk in, some guy in a dark suit fawning at me all serious before my eyes have a chance to adjust to the gloom.

Squinting, I say, "It's okay, pal. I'm not grieving anybody. I just brought a batch of boxes."

He looks at me. I mean, I must be white with sawdust, glue peeling like skin from my fingers. Not all that different from one of their corpses.

I'm still on the outdoor carpet runner, so I brush off a little. "Hot boxes," I explain, glancing around, seeing there is some kind of wake or something in progress. I lower my voice. "The things you burn them in."

"Are you with Buckfinch Construction?"

I give a nod, still hating to admit it after all these years. Hating not saying, "I'm with Rasmussen. Hell, I *am* Rasmussen."

"Out back," he whispers. "Not here!"

I nod again, peeking into the room, a lot of backs turned toward me, the coffin or urn or whatever—the main attraction—just out of sight beyond what I can see through the doorway. "Meet me out there?" I ask.

"There's a boy who will help you unload them."

I notice he's holding the door open for me and I step out into the sun alone, get myself turned around.

Around the side they've actually got loading doors, like they forklift the bodies in here in droves. Gives me a little case of the willies, really, till I realize they must be for the caskets, the real ones, big and heavy and expensive beyond anything that makes sense.

There's a kid raising the door before I even get the truck backed in. He's a high-schooler by the glimpse I catch; lanky and zit-faced, hair so blond it's white, cut short in a kind of Marine Corp stubble. I wonder what it does to him, working in there, at an age where the closest you should be getting to this kind of thing is parking out in the graveyard with your girlfriend. I wonder if his hair was that white before he started rolling bodies into a furnace that'd shame the fires of hell.

By the time I climb out from behind the wheel, the kid's already at the ropes, flinging them over the load where they coil limp on the concrete. I duck to miss the second one he heaves over, and yell, "Easy there, Flash. Got a guy in the hole over here." I cover my head with my hands and duck around the tailgate, hop up on the dock, ready to help. But just the way this guy attacked the ropes I know he's done this before and, knowing Bucky, he's done it himself. I bet Bucky never even got out of the cab, never once said boo to this kid's face.

He's climbed up on top of the load somehow, the whole stack teetering like a house of cards, him nipping around, sliding a box off, twisting it around by the handholds. As he tips it down toward the dock I see that he doesn't know I'm there, that he thinks he's still working on his own.

He flinches back in surprise when he catches sight of me, ducking his head quick and giving this kind of wave for me to get out of the way. The box slips down, setting on its end, rocking there for a second. Another follows after it. In nothing flat, without anything past that one glance, that one dismissing wave, he's got the top four boxes all standing on their ends, wobbling, like maybe there's already somebody inside, somebody who doesn't want to stay in there. Doesn't want anything to do with that conveyor belt or any incinerators.

The kid leaps down, pulling a scrunched-billed ball cap out of his butt pocket and tugging it low over his stubble. Then he sticks each hand into the upper handholds on a pair of boxes and lifts them standing upright, teetering himself now as he carries them off to a wall at the far end of the building. I do likewise, following after him.

Watching his back, the straining young muscles in his forearms as the boxes tip awkwardly with his walk, I say, "Bet you Bucky never gets out of the truck, huh?"

The kid doesn't say a thing. Just sets his boxes down and does this spin move around me, pulling his ball cap down so there isn't a chance I'll see his face.

That gives me a hitch, and I stop a second, just watching after him. Once I catch up, we do the same on the next pair of boxes, the kid keeping ahead of me, so all I catch are the tremble of the wiry thin muscles in his back and arms, the glimpse of the top of his cap as he moves quick, studying the ground.

Carrying the last load, I say, "You mind showing me around a little? Never been inside one of these places."

He just goes on ahead of me.

Louder, I say, "Maybe we could torch an empty box, see how long it takes, what exactly does get left."

He reaches the wall, sets down his last pair of boxes. I thump down my own, hard, the empty place echoing a little with the hollow-box boom.

The kid does his spin, starts off for the truck.

"What the . . ." I begin, gaping. The kid's what, seventeen, eighteen? I mean, it's bad enough having my own wife treat me this way. Before I know what I'm doing I dash after him and get hold of his T-shirt, spinning him around. I'm yelling, "What are you, frigging deaf?"

He barks out that kind of half roar, half moan deaf people think is talking, then lifts his hands to his ears, shaking his head. As he lets them fall he tries hitting my arm away.

"Sorry," I say, letting my hand drop from his shirt, which is warm and damp after carrying the boxes.

"Sorry," I say again.

The kid retreats to the truck, hops down, and spools up the ropes, setting them in the bed. He slams the tailgate. Climbing onto the dock, he stands by the button, waiting to close the door behind me.

I shout, "Thanks." Then just stand there watching him.

"I'll be back with the second load," I say, raising two fingers.

He has his thumb up on the button.

"You want to ride along?" I say, pointing to the truck. "I'll get you lunch." I bring my hand to my mouth, like I'm eating.

The kid doesn't even blink.

I walk past, jump off the dock, then wave for him to follow. I wait at the side of the truck, but he just stands there, thumb on the button.

"Look," I say. "I'm sorry. About grabbing you."

Standing in the shadow of the loading bay, watching the edges of glinty blond stubble beneath the filthy cap, I get a shiver that goes right through me, a bone-cold you'd expect in a place like this.

"Look," I say again. "I think I'm losing my wife." I glance from the kid to the spotlessly clean bay, then back to the kid. "Maybe an affair or something."

The kid starts chewing on a nail of his free hand. He turns his head so slowly it would be possible to miss it, until I can't see the slightest trace of his face.

"Do you know what I'm talking about?" I say, my voice up, but not because he can't hear. I feel like climbing up and grabbing him by the shirt again, spinning him around and shouting into his face until he understands.

Instead, I take a breath and only say, "Denise. Denise Roberts?" like he might know her by that name. "I first asked her out on a dare. We couldn't believe it when she said yes."

I pause, remembering months and months after that dare, out in the graveyard, Denise arching back to pull her T-shirt over her head; how she caught the way I looked at her and broke out laughing. "For Christ's sake," she'd said. "It's just me."

Then she'd pointed to her middle, where the lowest rib pressed against her smooth, warm skin. Just touching her made it hard for me to breathe. "Look at this," she said, sounding disgusted, running her finger along the rib. "It sticks out like a keel. But there's this operation I read about, where they can take out the rib." She twisted, naked before me, showing how she thought it would improve her profile. I reached up and pulled her down, holding her as tight as I could in my pickup in the middle of a graveyard.

Suddenly the deaf kid turns, looking right at me, almost as if he's been listening, peeking straight into that old pickup.

"We were going to have a baby," I say, but a motor groans out, chains clattering as the door starts coming down. I step back automatically, watching until the door clamps shut on its rubber gasket, the kid sealed up tight by himself.

I've stepped out of the shadow, I realize, and the sun is that spring kind it feels good just standing in. Leaning against my empty truck, I wait a long time, letting the warmth soak into my jacket. Then, standing straight, I hunch my shoulders, tightening the fabric across my back like a massage, hoping that warmth will stay with me when I climb in and head out, looking for Denise.

Freezeout

Every Sunday of our lives we drove to town for waffles and coffee. Dad acted like it was this big treat, but really it was just the one day a week he put his foot down, did something we wanted, instead of going along with Mom and her odd notions of what people do. And, even though I saw through him, I loved those mornings, too. Strawberry waffles. With whipped cream. Dad and me and Mom. Dad and his girls, he'd say, though we both knew everything would have been better if I'd been a boy. Then it could have been just the two of us all the time.

Now, sitting alone with Mom in her kitchen, I ask if she remembers those Sunday mornings. For just a second, a little breather, I'd like for us to think of something nice.

But, without a pause, Mom answers, "It was his way of substituting for church," gazing toward the door like he might step back in this very second. "He was a very religious man in his way," she goes on. "I know you know that."

Dad? Religious? I bite back a guffawed *What?!* I never once heard Dad say a single good thing about any religion.

I reach across the table, tap Mom's hand with my finger. Draw her attention away from the door. "Mom," I say again. "You have got to listen to me." I hold her hand, squeeze it until her eyes meet mine.

"Okay, Mom. This time listen. Please. Dad did not just take a vacation, some sort of trip. Mom, Dad is gone."

She watches me and I whisper, "Probably a heart attack. Maybe a stroke." Tiny, hard flakes of snow flit against the narrow panes on each side of the door. "Probably caught him out in the middle of nowhere, searching for some bird or other. We'll have to wait till some hunter finds him now." It's not easy saying this, but Mom's got to come back around to the real world. "What we can't do is pretend he is coming back."

"I think, somehow, we're his religion," Mom says. "You and me. His family."

I let go of Mom's hand. Reach for my cigarettes instead, tap one out of the pack the way Dad used to, across the back of my hand.

When I was a kid, Dad only ever diverted the Sunday waffle expedition when he came up with a birdwatching outing for the two of us. Somehow, though he spent his life making himself invisible, acting as if Mom's notions were all right as rain, taking part in entire fantasies as if the whole world saw things her way, Dad could then walk out into the normal world to do nothing more than search for birds. She never followed him after the birds, and those were the only times he could bring himself to leave her. Instead of getting a hot waffle, getting sandwiched between him and Mom and their steaming cups of thick coffee, the two of us would be cramped into some blind, wearing identical brown canvas work coats, mud-caked, charcoal-gray wool pants—still my favorite clothes. We'd sit side by side, wind-blasted and freezing, watching a bunch of grouse strutting around for mates at four A.M.; riding a ground blizzard to Freezeout to see a million snow geese turn the wind white with their wings.

I light the cigarette and take a long pull. Holding the smoke, I watch Mom, see her settling in for the long haul, digging in to await his return. Instead of blowing any rings, the way Dad taught me, I let the smoke leak out. I rub my eyes like I haven't slept in a month. Since the day he disappeared.

Though I talk hard, try to shock her into accepting something closer to some version of the truth, I don't have it in me to say my guess is that they won't find his cold fingers just clutching his chest. Even I have to shake away the picture when I figure it's as likely they'll find his fingers still holding some trigger or other, his head a sad, ruined mess. Birds can't fly you away from your whole life. Not when what you're running from is admitting you've spent your life hiding from Mom, ignoring that there might have been something we could have done, something that would have helped us all.

Finally I glance at my watch and tell Mom I've got to get to work, that I'll check back in on my way home. Odds are she'll have dinner waiting for me, me filling in for Dad now. And odds are I'll wind up spending the night again. Have another breakfast like this one tomorrow.

She says, "Maybe he'll be back by the time you get home."

I want to scream. But I just murmur, "No, Mom, he won't." That's worn out before the day's begun.

Maybe he drove his truck into Freezeout before pulling the trigger. Maybe this whole vanishing charade was his idea of leaving Mom with something to hold on to; a hope instead of a corpse. Like thinking you'd done something right by throwing a life ring to someone bobbing in the middle of the ocean, instead of stopping your pleasure cruise long enough to pick them up.

By the time I get home—to Mom's house, I mean—I'm running on fumes. I kick off my orthopedics (twenty-six years old and I wear shoes like my grandmother's) and slide into the chair across from Mom at the kitchen table. It's like she hasn't moved since I left.

I want to ask if he called, just so she could see how ridiculous she's acting, but I'm too tired to start.

She smiles at me. "How'd things go at the hospital, Liss?" she asks. "You look about done in."

It's exactly the kind of thing she was always asking Dad. "How were things at the mill?" Like if she didn't remind us, we might possibly forget where we worked.

"Same old," I say, realizing too late that that was Dad's answer. "Same old."

She cracks us both a beer, like she always did with Dad, but then remembers to ask if I'd rather have wine.

I shake my head, though I barely sip the beer. It'd just finish me off.

Mom's been baking all day, keeping busy, which is a good sign, I figure, and the dinner gives me a little bit of a second wind. As she slices pie for me, calories I need like a hole in the head, I see it's peach, with the crumbly cinnamon topping; Dad's favorite.

"Mom," I say, blowing out a sigh.

"I'm not waiting," she says, defensive right away.

It gives me a shock. It's the closest she's come to making sense in this long month. "Good," I say.

"But think how he'll like it if he does come back right now. Finding this hot peach pie."

"Oh, Mom, for God's sake."

She looks down, carefully lifting both our pieces from the tin. She slides mine in front of me, fidgets with her own. "Ice cream?" she asks.

"No, Mom," I say. "Just this is too much."

"Don't be silly," she answers. "You're as slim as a weasel."

A weasel? I'm built like a truck. Like Dad. Solid, he used to say. "My rock." Like that was some kind of compliment.

But it's me, of all people, who suggests driving into town Sunday morning. It's usually a working day for me—sickness and accidents taking no vacations—but I'm at the end of a rotation, the days mixed up as ever.

Mom looks over at me. She's been dusting.

"Why not?" I say. "Maybe get a waffle."

She's slipping into her coat, tugging her hat down over her ears before I can find my checkbook.

"I should have thought of this myself," she tells me.

In the car, she claps my thigh as I'm backing out. "It was this easy!" she says.

I shift into drive and look over at her, the familiar queasy feeling rising in my belly. "What, Mom? What have you got yourself thinking?"

"It's Sunday, Liss. Of course that's where he'll be. He's probably been there every Sunday, wondering what's keeping us."

I start slowly down the road. "Mom," I say. "You got to stop. People will start wondering."

She gives her tiny laugh. "I'm used to that, honey. That doesn't bother me at all."

Well, couldn't it? I want to shout, every time I didn't invite over someone who might have been my friend rushing back in on me. I take a breath. "Mom," I say, "if he ran off, why would he be waiting for us?" The one thing I always did was talk to Mom like she was no different than the rest of us, just a little slow on the uptake, needing things explained once or twice more. The way Dad went along with whatever she dreamed up made me want to slap him.

Mom keeps looking out the window, smiling. "I should have changed," she says. "Worn something a little nicer."

"Mom. Why do you think he ran away in the first place?" Dad had the most ironclad routines on the planet. If he didn't show up for dinner, you could count on it, he was dead.

"Honestly," Mom says. "I wore these same clothes yesterday. I've become some sort of hillbilly. He won't like that."

"Mom!" I shout.

She turns to me, as if surprised to find anyone driving the car at all.

"If he ran away from us, why would he be waiting?"

"He didn't run away from us," she answers, as if it were as plain as the road before us.

I'm interested. She's never offered a theory. But when she doesn't go on, I have to prompt, "Why then?"

"You'll have to ask him, honey. Honestly, I could never tell what went on in that man's mind."

I can't keep from blurting, "What do you think he thought went on in *yours*?" but Mom's got the visor mirror down, pushing at her hair.

"When he knelt beside our bed every night, praying so hard the sweat stood on his forehead, I would ask, 'What are you praying for, Erling? What more could you possibly want?' But he would only smile and slip in beside me. 'Nothing, Emma,' he'd answer. 'Only giving thanks.' "

By the time we reach the coffee shop, I'm convinced I've made a huge mistake. Mom has her odd notions, but she's not out-and-out nuts. At least not till Dad left. This religion thing—Dad on his knees praying. I trudge up the steps, hold the door for her, afraid of what might happen once we're inside, only the two of us.

Nothing happens. Of course he's not there, but Mom acts like that's just what she expected.

"Let's sit by the window, Liss," she says. "So we can see him coming."

I drop down beside her, wishing they had something stronger we could put in the coffee.

She keeps fiddling with herself, preening without a mirror, waiting on him. We drink gallons. She orders a waffle that sits cold and solid between us, neither of us able to muster the courage to take a bite. Finally I have to say, "Look, Mom, I'm sorry I brought you down here. This was a world-record bad idea."

"Oh, you know how he is," she says quickly. "Always late."

Dad was never late in his life. Count on him like a clock.

"He forgot our very first date together," Mom says out of the blue. "Stood up! I have never been so angry."

This is another I've never heard before. "What happened?"

"He called the very next day. Saturday. Introduced himself and asked if I'd like to do something next Friday. 'I don't know,' he said. 'Maybe a movie.'

" 'Erling Nilsen!' I hissed. 'I would rather date a snake!' " Mom giggles. "That's just what I told him."

"Really?"

"Completely forgot we had a date the night before. Oh, he could be so absentminded."

"I never saw that, Mom. Not once."

"There were years and years before you, Liss. You haven't been with us long at all."

Twenty-six years, I think. Poof. A little waffle-gobbling interruption.

It's almost noon before Mom lets me talk her out of the coffee shop. She says he must have gone out to the lake. "Sure," she says. "It's November, the last of the geese will still be there. I'm sure he's out there, saying good-bye."

If only he had said good-bye, I think. How much easier it would have been. But I don't think he ever got accused of gross bravery. Not Dad. Not our Birdman.

I say, "Sure, Mom, that's probably what's going on. He's been at the lake for a month." I don't mention that it's fall, hunting season; that Dad couldn't stand being out there with the guns echoing off the hills, when every now and then you could see a piece of white separate itself from the flocks and plummet down, crashing into the weeds and the water. Seconds later you'd hear the shot, another harmless-sounding boom, just like all the rest. The only time he took me out in the fall I just gaped at all those staggering, collapsing geese. He caught me watching, almost ready to cry, and he tugged me back to the car so fast I couldn't follow him from hummock to hummock and I wound up filling my boots with the rotting black water. He drove in a fury, and I hid my ruined socks beneath the car seat, shoving them back as far as I could, wondering what I'd done so wrong.

Back in Mom's kitchen, I have to tell her I've got an afternoon shift. I can't stand being cooped up here with her all day.

Right away she says, "I thought you were off today? The end of your rotation?" sniffing out a lie the way she always could, no matter how far off you thought she'd wandered.

"I'm filling in for Annie," I say, just as quick, ready to spin out explanations that'd exhaust anybody before they could dig clear to the truth. "Her kid is sick."

"Which one?"

"Emmett," I answer. "Another ear infection. She's afraid they'll have to tube it."

We eye each other, each knowing the other's talents, seeing there'll be no winner here.

It's only lunchtime, but I follow the river back into town and sit at a bar, the one Dad and I used to stop at on our way home from the birds, stalling I knew, though Dad said he only wanted to catch the football scores. I watch a couple of plays of the game that's on; somebody against Denver. John Elway and his big white teeth. I order a beer, but the place is so full of men I wind up leaving before I'm done. I don't even like beer.

Crossing the parking lot, the wind whistles through me like always, and I sit a second in the car, catching my breath, wondering what to do next. I wonder how many times Dad did this, escaping Mom. I rub my arms around myself, chilled to the bone. It's been a hard winter already, and it's not even Thanksgiving. The idea of the holidays, without the routine of Dad, gives me a whole new shiver.

I drive aimlessly at first, down by the tracks and the old brewery, the hardscrabble sections, paint-peeling shacks alternating with 1960s mobile homes, a few swayback horses penned in little squares of frozen mud. Country music strongholds.

You can only take so much of that, and before I know it I'm on the highway, driving fast enough I've got a fair chance of winding up in my own emergency room. The heater's blowing on high, the fan buzzing on the leaves caught in the vents, but I'm clear to Sun River before I quit shivering, before I take the turn to Freezeout.

Mom's right. If Dad was anyplace, it'd be out looking for the last of the year's birds. Maybe hunting season's over.

I drive through Fairfield, proudly the Malting Barley Capital of the World. What title could we claim, I wonder; what capital would our family be? The Missing Persons Capital of the World? Maybe. Mom's barely here. And me, I guess I've worked pretty hard at not leaving any tracks, hardly a shadow. If I vanished today, only Mom'd much care, and she'd just settle in that much deeper, waiting on the day Dad and I both returned, unbothered by any doubts of the outcome. Dad's the easy one in the family. He's just plain missing.

The lake, when I come around the turn and shoot over the railroad tracks, is stretched out below me. Though the day is low and steely, the surface is all glimmery white. For a second I think, Wow, they're all still here, every goose in the world. But then I realize it's ice, that the whole place is already frozen over. There isn't a hunter's trailer or tent to be seen. Not a living thing.

I slow to a crawl, then bump over a cattle guard and edge past the deserted headquarters building. The wind, twice as strong here as in town, rocks my car on its springs. If I hurt myself out here, I think, I wouldn't last long. They'd find me the same time as Dad, in the spring thaw. I'd leave a note, I think, a double-suicide I'd call it. Let Mom figure out a way to weave that into whatever goes on in her head.

I haven't stopped here since the day of the dying geese, half my life ago, but now it's like I've never been away. If Dad walked out of the clump of trees beside me, I wouldn't even flinch. Just throw the door open for him, crank the heater back to full blast, and ask him what he thought about there, away from us so long. Just what exactly he thought he was doing leaving Mom to wait like that, if he thought that was some kind of mercy. Maybe, at last, I'd get him to admit to cowardice.

I inch down the rutted, frost-crusted road to the edge of the lake, to a ramp where the hunters unload their boats, but there's no water to be seen. The lake is pewter gray in its dull armor of ice, broken near shore, jumbles of different blocks angling over each other. Chaos stilled. Wind eddies snatch wisps of snow out of the reeds, whirling them across the hard, slick top.

Dad could be under any of it. Surprised-looking and stiff, fingers around what? Chest? Binoculars? Trigger?

For a while, at work, I kept expecting him to be trundled off the latest ambulance. Maybe even the helicopter. He'd like that, I'd think, a helicopter ride; finally getting a bird's-eye view of everything that had surrounded him for so long. Funny thing to hope, I guess, that your father will show up in emergency.

In the trunk I've got the standard Montana-winter package—sand, shovel, chains, blankets, boots. I pull the release from inside, and after one last bracing breath, I dash out, snagging the boots and blankets and an extra wool cap that, as soon as I'm back in the car, I see is one of Dad's. Like we've already divided his belongings among the survivors.

I leave the boots down by the heater, warming the felt liners before slipping my feet inside. I tug Dad's hat low around my head, then pull my collar above it, sealing out the wind. Finally I wrap the blankets around me, like some old picture of reservation Indians, huddling into themselves and their government blankets, everything around them so unknown.

When I step out, the wind flaps the blankets around me like wings—big, gray goose wings; Canadas, not snows. I step onto the ice, where the water would only be inches deep, and head into the wind. If I walk around the whole lake, it'll be at my back half the time anyway.

It's not as if I expect to find anything. With the freezes and thaws we've already had, and the black water, and the snow, the ice is like steel, not glass. I could walk right over him and not know. He could be under there watching me, calling my name, and I'd walk right on, blinded by the ice, deafened by the wind. But somehow I think I'll know. If I find him, I'll know.

But just realizing what I'm thinking, how goofy it is, I have to raise a hand and wipe the tears from my cheeks. Maybe it's only the wind, but I'm suddenly so afraid I've finally become my mother—my mind leap-frogging and whirling that same way—I can barely see. I stagger on, holding my hand out to brush the reeds, keeping myself from wandering out too far, where the ice might not be solid, where I might vanish from the face of the earth.

Halfway around the lake, the wind's lashing the side of my face, my body stiff with its cold, my hearing numbed by the constant rattle and clash of the frozen reeds. The isolation is womblike somehow, but all wrong; the world nothing but white noise, dirty white sky, dirty white ice; no place where one ends and the other begins. Not a womb you'd ever want anything coming out of.

But as I wind through the turn, stumbling on the broken, lumpy ice, the wind begins to nudge me forward, pushing at me, urging me on. It's scary, and I don't want to find what it wants me to see.

I stop.

Shaking my head, I rub my mittens hard against my face. My nose is running, and I wipe at it like a kid, leaving a long silvery streak across the back of the wool. Now that I'm not moving, the wind pushes harder, more insistently.

What the wind wants me to see? I think. *Not wanting anything coming out of this womb?* I've gone way past anywhere Mom ever thought of going. I could go back home and give her lessons on how to let her mind run away.

I rub my face even harder, and then lift my head and shout out my name—"Melissa!"—just to let myself know I'm here, that I'm not completely gone.

"You're probably getting hypothermic," I say out loud. "Your brain is freezing." Then, "I'm talking to myself, Mom. Aren't you proud?"

I let the wind shuffle me along again. But now I'm only heading back to the car, not looking for something I'll never find. I tell myself this, but not out loud. I'm not crazy, I say. This was worth a look. This is the kind of place Dad would come to pray.

I have to stop to climb over the leaning remains of a fence I find poking out of the reeds. The wind makes it hard to balance, to keep from snagging any of the nasty, rusted barbs, each one tetanus waiting to happen. With one leg over, my hands pressing the wires away from my legs, I notice the sign on the near post: HUNTING CLOSURE AREA, NO HUNTING BEYOND THIS POINT.

This is where Dad'd be, I think. Hiding out here away from the guns. I wonder if I should break through the reeds, try to find some ground, some road, some dip that might have hidden his truck all this time. But somebody would have had to have seen it, right? Some airplane? Some game warden making a last sweep after the lake froze over?

I get my other leg over the wire and let the fence go, jerking my hands away before the barbs can snag the wool of my mittens. Snapping back, the wire makes a loud, whistling twang, a ricochet kind of noise.

But even before the wind whisks away the wire's screech, there's a new sound; a crackling, rushing commotion in the reeds, close, moving fast, breaking things. Scared senseless, I fall into a crouch, bringing my hands up to protect my face, though the only thing I can imagine is that it must be Dad, rushing to scoop me into his arms as soon as he found me searching for him.

Then, before I realize it couldn't be Dad, before I can even take a breath, a snow goose breaks free of the reeds that have hidden it, sheltered it from the wind. Not ten feet away.

It thrashes away from me, one wing flapping hard while the other drags sloppily across the ice, catching on the last stalks of broken reeds poking through. It's the same dirty white of the sky and the ice, except for the startling black flashes of its wing tips, the open orange surprise of its bill as it honks and honks, left behind and doomed.

"Stop!" I shout, as if it will listen, as if it will let me care for it, mend it as I would any broken person.

But the goose just keeps flailing across the lake, the wind drifting it sideways, and I stand watching it, finally feeling the crushing weight of Dad's love. For both of us. Mom and me.

The wind eddies around me, an obstacle, flapping my blankets, blowing the goose into a reaching finger of reeds a quarter-mile in front of me. I can barely see it then, just the black tips of its wings as it tries to fold them back into place. The one still drags, and I see its black end bob as the goose crawls over the lumps of reeds and disappears again, hiding from what can't be much longer in coming.

Then, slowly, I begin picking my own way through the reeds, looking for land, for the roads I remember creeping down with my father when we left Mom at home, alone with her ideas.

The road, somehow, is right where I pictured it being, a pair of ruts in the grass, smudged with what snow there is, caught in the depressions, falling out of the wind. I walk in the center hump, the short, brittle grass crackling under my feet, on my way back home to Mom. I keep myself from searching the snow for anyone's tracks. I'm not looking for Dad anymore. I'm only trying to circle the goose, not drive it out again, give it what peace it has left.

Black Tie and Blue Jeans

When I finally get close to her, all I come up with is, "Can you believe this winter?" The weather, for crying out loud.

But she looks at me as if I said something like, "So, this Milosevic character, if it weren't for this damned election, being recalled from our embassy, I think I could have nudged him in the right direction." Or, "I've just been going over the figures, and if we aren't in for a major readjustment on Wall Street, well, then I never did make my millions on the floor."

I mean, she just gapes at me. I figure she must think I'm somebody else, someone she's met before and can't remember where, or who.

But believe me, we haven't met before. She isn't somebody I'd forget for even a second.

Wall Street. I own the fading hamburger drive-in by the interstate. I've got eight grand split between two mutual funds. Eight percent on one, worse on the other. There's two thousand squirreled away in an IRA I haven't added to since that first burst of responsibility. My life's savings.

With her still gazing up at me, I have to say something else, and I start with, "Colder than," but all the colder-thans I know start stacking up in my mouth—than a well digger's . . . than a brass monkey's . . . than a witch's . . . —and I wind up stammering out, "Colder than cold."

It's hopeless. Like I knew it'd be the first time I saw her from across the room, just a slice of chestnut hair bouncing off a perfect smooth line of neck, a flash of bare shoulder.

The Chamber of Commerce sent a free ticket for this shindig to the drive-in, not even addressed to me, though I've owned the place going on fifteen years now, standing guard through its decline since the heyday fifties. This party's an annual event, a fund-raiser for the symphony of all things. Very schmoozy. It's the first ticket I've ever seen, and I have a suspicion the whole thing's a mistake. But I thought, What have I got to lose, and marked it down on my calendar, as if I might otherwise lose it in the rush of social engagements. BTBJ, I wrote. For black tie and blue jeans. What they call the party. A name I find so embarrassingly hick, so Great Falls, I can't spell it out.

But, once I was here, once I saw her hair, I maneuvered for a further look. Believe me, I didn't have to break off any conversations. I've lived here my whole life, except for the college stint, where I somehow missed the vital step of acquiring a wife, but at this party, in my requisite black jacket and tie, my brand-new, stiff-as-a-board blue jeans, I could count the people I knew on one hand.

Catching further glimpses through the arms and legs, the fancy dresses and black jackets, I saw the side of her face, still perfect as far as I could see. Finally a glimpse lower down, my pulse doing crazy things. Even her legs—the last look I had before blundering so close I had to say, "Can you believe this winter?"—tapered beautifully into black stiletto heels.

This whole rundown, as embarrassing as it is to think of, is something I always do. As if I'm some kind of connoisseur, the kind of guy who would cast aside a beautiful woman over a thick ankle. Me, with my hamburgers straddling my waist, my forehead growing longer every year. If she hadn't turned right into me, I never would have said a word.

I'm wearing a black Stetson now to hide the forehead. The jacket goes a long way to keeping the waist a secret. A lot farther than the grease-flecked apron I wear when I fill in for a missing cook.

Finally, ignoring the weather completely, she says, "I know you, don't I?"

"I know you couldn't," I say. "I'd remember you." I stop myself there.

She puts a finger on her chin, eyeing me too closely. She doesn't say, "I never forget a face," which makes me wonder if there's a reason she remembers mine, from what could only have been a glimpse through a mostly menu-covered window. Maybe something she saw that she liked.

"I never come to these things," I say.

She keeps studying me, beginning to tap the edge of her teeth with the tip of her fingernail.

I can't keep a nervous smile from starting. I say, "If I have to shovel out from under one more storm, I'm going to be a coronary statistic."

Suddenly she grins, a huge open smile that draws me right in. I feel like laughing. "What?" I say.

"With cheese," she says. "No onions. And a huckleberry shake. You're Mr. Blackthorn!"

"How do you know that?" I ask. It's not like I work the cars.

"I used to work there when I was a girl," she says. "We all did."

I have been sucked across the room by an ex-employee, and up beneath my cowboy hat I feel my forehead flush crimson. A high school carhop. But she couldn't have been a girl farther than fifteen years back, and I say, "I know all the girls who—"

She gives a funny little whoop, passing her hand up over her face and across her hair. "Boy, we all had such crushes on you back then." She fails to choke back a laugh, her grin huge.

I feel sweat around my collar, in my palms, though knowing this woman once had a crush on me is better news than I've had in a long time.

"I'm sorry I don't remember you," I stammer. "There's been an awful lot of girls there." About five a year, I think, none lasting longer than that. Cigarette money, maybe beer. A place to be seen. The one girl, a heavyset, lonely, pimply kid who worked her way through college there, is still a legend. It's not a career move.

"How could you remember me?" she says, still laughing, actually reaching out and grabbing my elbow for an instant, giving it a tiny shake. "That was eons ago."

She stares at me again. "I don't even want to think how I looked back then. I'm flattered you can't remember."

"I'm flattered too," I say. "About the crush." I glance at my feet, her ankles. "I never knew that."

"No?" she says. She actually bats her eyes. "All of us. You were our dream man."

"A drive-in owner?" I ask.

"We were in high school," she says. "We didn't care what you did. You couldn't have been more than a few years older than us. Just perfect. Sophisticated. Handsome. Rich."

I try to smile. "I bought the place right after college," I tell her. "My dad was sick—dying, really—and he helped with the money. To keep me close, I suppose."

She sticks out her hand, still giving that wide open grin. "I'm Gina," she says. "Gina Natron. Though, in those old days it was Bateman."

Neither name means a thing to me, but I'd checked for a ring. First chance I had. A divorce?

"Blackie," I say, taking her hand, shaking it as long as seemly. "People call me Blackie."

"Blackie," she repeats.

"What are you doing now?" I ask. I grin myself. "Don't tell me you've gone over to the other side. You're not slapping out Ramp Burgers at Boyd's?"

She laughs again, something I'd tail her around this whole party just to hear.

"No, no. I'm just a stay-at-home." She gives a backhand wave toward a group of black jackets, generic country-clubbers hobnobbing over highball glasses. "Darren sells farm insurance. He just landed a contract with Anheuser-Busch. Crop damage for their barley growers."

I nod, but she smiles, guessing at or actually seeing the glaze creep over my face.

"I know," she says. "But you wouldn't believe the money involved."

I smile. "Not many people recognize the same thing about the burger industry. My cash flow?" I shake my head. "Whooee."

She laughs again, but not like before.

After a second or two, I let out a big breath. "So," I say. "Kids?"

She shakes her head. "We still hope."

I nod, and we look away from each other, smiling pleasantly, suddenly interested to see how the party is going.

Before I know what I'm doing, I dig out my wallet, nearly skinning my knuckles on my rock-hard blue jeans. I slip out a drive-in freebie card and, finding a pen in my jacket, I sign the bottom line, making it official, then, without allowing myself to think, I scribble my phone number underneath.

"Here you go, Gina. Not just anybody gets one of these." I'm stuffing a stack of them back into my wallet.

She waves the card between us. "The other girls on the cheerleading squad will just die!" she says.

Then she glances back to the group of men. "I better check in," she says.

I nod, smile, hold out my hand again. "Good seeing you," is all I find to say.

Her hand lingers in mine. "I can taste that huckleberry shake already," she says. Then she waves, over her shoulder, all her fingers up and down at the same time, very cheerlead-erish. "See you at the malt shop," she says, turning around, heading to her husband.

Watching her go, I feel a way I haven't felt since high school. Happy, but afraid, vaguely embarrassed. The odds suddenly seem high that, while I was talking to her, feeling myself breaking through the crust of the party and really making contact, I was being laughed at, the joke apparent to everyone but me. Mr. Blackthorn. "I told him we all had crushes on him!" More giggling girlish laughter.

After watching her husband accept her into the fold of his arm, I leave the party, stepping into the biting teeth of the winter that had been so on my mind. I haul my black collar as tight around my neck as it will go, run with slithering steps out to my car, afraid of the ice and snow.

I drive straight to the drive-in, closed now for an hour and a half, though, in truth, I should close it all winter, cutting my losses. The romance of hanging a tray on your window while a cute high school girl bounces out with your milkshake loses something when she's bundled up like an Eskimo crone, when the frost crusts so thick inside your windows you have to scrape it off before you can drive away.

Inside it's warm, close and greasy- smelling. Using only the faint glow of the neon root beer sign I leave on all night, I dig through the order forms, the suppliers' catalogs. And finally I find it, the Kalispell distributor who sells the huckleberries for the shakes. I haven't sold those in years, and I wonder if he's still in business.

I tear off his phone number and stuff it in the inside pocket of my best black jacket. My only one. Tomorrow, first thing, I'll call in an order for the huckleberries. Then I'll call my fry cook and give him the bad news, something I've put off too long already. "Cutting my losses," I'll tell him, feeling guilty. "It's not something I have any choice about."

I'll take over the job myself. Actually working out here every day. The huckleberries all ready to add to the ice cream. Just in case.

But as I step back out into the icy night, I see my waist-line growing larger yet as I eat those huckleberry shakes alone, dreaming of Wall Street, of foreign assignments. I sink my neck deeper into my collar and shuffle across the ice to my car, the only one in the vacant row before the huge painted menu. I reach my own window and lean down, ready to take any kind of order, but the only face looking back in the frosted glass is my own.

Willowy-Wisps

As they drove past the dunes lining the gray shore, Alston began to tell the policeman about the Dismal Swamp. Alston had never heard of the swamp before last night and he really didn't know much about it. There were no dunes there, but huge, heavy, thick trees. "The air was so wet and dark it seemed hard to breathe," he said. There was a ghostly smell of old things there too, and Alston forgot to talk as he recalled that dank reek.

Then he said, "I didn't pay much attention to the swamp, I guess. It was a spooky place. Lonely. But I was with Margie, you know." He'd thought that with Margie there was nothing in the world that could've been lonely. After a moment, Alston added, "You don't know Margie."

He paused then, just breathing. He'd taken Margie out to the swamp in his father's truck, just the two of them on the long ride, skipping the Homecoming game, the dance; tall tales sown everywhere to hide their absence. After their stop in

Elizabeth City he'd seen the swamp on the map. Right then he'd liked the name of it, and he thought the swamp would be an empty place where they could have privacy. It was that, but that hadn't brought anything he'd thought it would.

"It was hot," Alston said to the policeman. "Soon as we left Wilkesboro it was hot. Even hotter than it is now. We rolled the windows down and we could barely hear ourselves think." A moment later he added, "The muffler was shot, but that was sort of fun."

They'd stopped and bought Cokes at a service station, glad for the moments in the shade. He had looked at her then in her pale sundress, already sticking to her in the heat. When she saw how he looked at her she smiled but got back into the truck where he couldn't see.

"It made me feel like somebody," Alston said. "Somebody like you maybe. Buying gas for the truck with Margie waiting for me so we could get back on the road. We'd fixed it so we could stay out all night." Alston remembered that although they'd made those plans, they had sidestepped any mention of what they might mean. "We were going to the ocean. To the Outer Banks. Neither of us had ever seen the ocean. We wanted to do it together.

"I tried to get a motel room in Elizabeth City," he said. He could still barely believe he'd done that. Without even asking Margie first. "I figured we could go out to the ocean in the morning that way," he told the policeman. "See the sunrise." Alston shook his head and squirmed a little, trying to get his cuffed wrists comfortable behind him. The policeman glanced at him in the rearview mirror and Alston smiled shyly, still shaking his head.

"She didn't even let me get out of the truck," he said. "She said just because we were going to spend a night out didn't mean we were married. She said now she wasn't even sure she wanted to marry me. She said she didn't know that at all, if that's all I had on my mind."

Alston stared at the sluggish, ceaseless swells. "She was nervous is all. Nervous as I was. That wasn't all I had on my mind.

"On the way out all we talked about was the ocean. She looked at the map and saw that Kitty Hawk was out there. She asked if that wasn't where the Wright brothers had flown. I said sure it was. And she said, 'I want to see that. I want to see where people first learned to fly. Maybe there's something there that gave them the idea.' She hugged me. She said, 'Maybe we could learn something like that.'

"When she got mad at the motel I wished I'd asked her what she meant by that. But now she wouldn't talk about any of it. Like staying one night in a motel could keep her from ever learning to fly."

Alston had driven to the swamp from Elizabeth City. It was only a few miles, but it wasn't like the trip over from Wilkesboro. The adventure had been swallowed by silence and he'd grown angry, even when she moved back next to him as they drove.

"She finally took my arm and put it around her," he whispered. "It was nice again and we started to talk and we decided we'd go to Virginia, see the ocean from there. It would've been the first time we'd been to another state."

Alston tugged at the cuffs and turned to try to sit sideways in the seat. He watched the policeman through the heavy grille caging, waiting for him to glance at him again. When he didn't look away from the road, Alston said, "But it got dark as we were driving through the middle of the swamp and we saw the lights. We stopped to look."

Alston remembered the eerie way the lights had shimmered on and off, rather than flashing. "There were greeny ones and kind of bluer ones," he said, "though none of them were very bright. They never stayed in one place long either. We couldn't ever pin them down." It was dark and Margie had nestled in tighter to his side and asked about them.

"Margie didn't know what they were," Alston said. "I told her they were will-o'-the-wisps. My grandma used to call them that. We'd see them once in a while in the hollows.

"Margie didn't get it right, though," Alston said. "She called them willowy-wisps." He'd laughed at that and then they'd kissed. He told her, whispering, that they were the spirits of dead people, trying to get them to follow them into the swamp, where they would get lost and die. She had slapped him gently, saying he was scaring her. He didn't believe that for a second and he hugged her harder and laughed again and said willowy-wisps, raising his voice up high, like hers. She had slapped at him again but he had caught her wrist that time and held it, and they kissed again, for a long time, doing everything they'd done before, driving themselves crazy with the stopping.

Alston remembered how, as they kissed and squirmed, the shoulders of her dress kept slipping off, how finally she didn't bother putting them back, even as he slid them lower yet. The satiny touch of her breasts, at last without the intervening layers of shirt and bra, was something he could still nearly feel on his fingers. As soon as he'd seen her in that dress he knew it didn't allow for a bra and the mere idea had made it hard to think during the entire drive.

When he tried to slide the dress lower still, she'd pushed him up just far enough to say, "Alston," her lips so close they brushed his face. "No," she said. Then, "Alston, don't," but beneath the cloth, he'd brushed the naked flatness of her belly, and he heard how her breath sucked in, how she trembled as his fingers edged beneath the slim stretchy band of her under-wear, how she pushed tighter against him. It made it impossible

to move his hand, and she said, "Alston, please," but he lifted
up enough to wriggle his hand lower yet. She ground back up
against him, again pinning his hand, but Alston was already
stunned by the heat and wetness he'd discovered.

When he raised up enough to slip her dress all the way off,
Margie hadn't said a word. She barely lifted her bottom, letting
him slide the dress down her legs, a tiny scooch that made it
hard for Alston to breathe.

Then he'd opened his own pants, Margie turning her head
away, closing her eyes. "Alston," she'd said, her whisper shaking over his name as if she were pleading.

In the back of the squad car Alston had grown quiet, staring
out at the colorless flat line of the ocean's edge. When he
caught the policeman glancing around at him he didn't smile.
He said, "That's not all I wanted."

Margie had cried afterward. She opened the truck door and
he'd run out after her, afraid for her with the snakes that would
come to the warm road. But she hadn't left the truck. She was
leaning with her back to the rusty bed, hooking the shoulders
of her dress back over her arms, which were even paler than
the cloth.

She wasn't crying anymore. That had only lasted a second,
but she would not return his hug when he held her. He told
her he loved her. She looked up at him then and wiped the
tears from her face. "That doesn't prove anything," she had
said, and now Alston repeated that out loud.

The policeman sat straighter. "What doesn't prove anything?" he asked.

Alston looked at him but didn't answer. He stared out the
window again, not so far this time, but just past the dunes, at
the fat, heavy swells of the ocean they'd come so far to see.

The next words she'd said were, "Take me home." When

he tried to remind her of the elaborate trail they'd left behind so they could spend the night together, she'd simply repeated, "Take me home."

"That's the last thing she said, 'Take me home,' " Alston said, as if he had just realized it. As he'd turned the truck around and started to drive he'd been acutely aware of it, feeling lonelier than he had ever felt in his life, with her not three feet away, but drawn up into herself stiff and hard and silent.

The world around them had been as black as anything he had ever known and the muffler roared and the headlights didn't light up enough of anything. He didn't understand any of it. He didn't understand what all his friends' sex bragging had been about, and now he didn't even understand why he had been so anxious to do that with Margie. And he didn't understand what had gone wrong and why she wouldn't even pretend to talk to him.

He hadn't been dying to talk himself. But it seemed he couldn't understand anything alone. Least of all why what they had just done had changed everything so much for the worse, when it wasn't supposed to do that at all. In all their talk, his friends never said a word about anything like this. After being that close he was more alone than he had ever been, and he didn't have any idea who was riding next to him in the truck. In the reflection from the road her face shone like broken stone, a mask or a shield.

"I kept asking her what was wrong," Alston said. "But she just sat there, looking worse and worse."

"Then what happened?" the policeman said and for a moment their eyes met in the mirror.

"You know what happened then," Alston said. He didn't like this policeman as much as he wanted to. When he'd first pulled him over, even pointed his gun straight at Alston, the only thing Alston could feel was relief. Relief that it was over; relief that he wasn't alone anymore.

Alston closed his eyes, sick from watching the swells break against the shore like great, dark blisters. When she wouldn't talk he'd finally pulled over and said, "Look, Margie, we're okay. Nothing's changed."

"Maybe for you it hasn't," she'd said. "I don't even know that anymore."

"Yes you do!" he'd answered. He sat and stared at her while she glared straight ahead. She was making him angry again and when he said, "Margie, I'm gonna take a little walk," he barely avoided saying it through his teeth. "I'm gonna take a little walk. Just down the road and back. Maybe you'll think better when I'm not here bothering you. Maybe you can think of something to say next time I ask you what's wrong. Okay?" When she hadn't answered, hadn't even looked at him, he said, "Okay, Margie?"

When she said, "Just take me home," Alston said, "I'm going to take this walk first. And then you're going to tell me what went so wrong." His teeth were clenched. "I want to know what we did that was so wrong, Margie."

His door screeched when he opened it, loud in the still night. In the distance the yard light of some solitary house shone brightly. Alston had pulled over when he saw it, figuring they were out of the swamp now, probably getting close to a town. He couldn't remember for sure. On the way out here things had been going well. Margie had been against his shoulder, close enough to whisper nice things and still be heard over the roar of the truck.

He'd slammed his door a little harder than he meant to, and the dead smell of the swamp surrounded him. He remembered the quick bile-taste of fear when Margie had jumped out and he'd thought of all the snakes drawn to the road. At first he walked quickly toward the swamp, almost hoping a snake would make his next move for him. But then he thought of dying out here from a cottonmouth bite and missing everything that he and Margie would do forever and he started to walk more slowly, shuffling his feet for the noise it made. He even started to hum, letting the snakes know he was coming.

He was still thinking about snakes when he heard the truck's engine fire, roaring like a blast furnace in the empty night. He whirled around and saw the headlights blaze a path in the darkness and he heard the tearing grind of gears and a little squeal of tires and the engine dying. He started to run but she got the truck going again and this time she screeched out without killing it, driving in a determinedly straight line away from him. The ground was flat and the road was straight and Alston stopped running, watching her lights a long time after they had disappeared.

Minutes passed before Alston forced his legs to move again. He shuffled along, though he didn't remember to think of snakes. He looked at the yard light ahead, maybe a mile, though in the darkness it was hard to tell anything for sure.

When he looked back down at the road he found that the light had blinded him. He stumbled off the shoulder and long reeds slithered away from his face and warm, thick water wrapped around his ankles. He was sure he could feel hundreds of slick coils tightening around him and he scrambled frantically back to the hard, smooth surface of the asphalt, wildly out of breath.

Alston waited until he stopped shaking, then held his hand out before him, blocking the light. He concentrated on keeping his feet on the road, feeling for the shoulder through the toe of his tennis shoe. The croakings of millions of frogs rose like thunder from the swamp and an occasional will-o'-the-wisp flickered at the edge of his vision, disappearing if he turned to see.

The house wasn't as far away as it had appeared in the

trickery of the swamp's night air. He walked up the gravel drive, listening to the frogs and the crunch of stone under his soft, wet shoes. He braced himself for the rush of any dogs and crossed through the light to the porch. The doorbell echoed through the house. He rang it again, and again.

Alston stood on the porch, wondering why he hadn't noticed the frogs earlier. When he had been with Margie he'd hardly noticed anything. He wondered if she would come back for him, after she'd cooled down, and he sat to wait it out. But the frogs' noise grew louder and louder and he pictured the snakes out there, slithering toward them. With only the light of the willowy-wisps the frogs wouldn't have a chance.

Alston looked around the darkness, wondering again about dogs. The night was suddenly so full of sound he realized he wouldn't be able to hear the dogs, wouldn't know they were there until they were upon him, tearing at him. He stood quickly, turning to the harsh glare of the yard light and the worn truck that sat under it.

Alston took a step toward the truck. Waiting for Margie was what his mother would call a fool's errand. Margie had turned into something brand-new, something he didn't know the first thing about.

"Do you know what a fool's errand is?" Alston asked the policeman.

The policeman glanced into the mirror and shook his head. "Why don't you tell me?" he said.

Suddenly Alston realized the policeman was trying to trick him into saying things that would look bad later, that he'd been doing that the whole trip. He stared at the policeman, but they were in town now, and the policeman had to keep his eyes on the road.

Watching the people on the sidewalks, Alston remembered how alone he'd been as he'd walked toward that truck. He'd felt as if he might soon be nothing but one of those wavery old wisps of light. The ghost of a dead person. The idea made him feel as if he was smothering. He thought of Margie racing down some road in the blackness, all alone herself, but with her face still that hard and blank, as if she'd been looking for just this solitude all her life.

Alston had run the last steps to the truck. He was out of breath again, as out of breath as he'd been when he'd blundered into the edge of the swamp. The yard light shone full on the keys dangling from a baling-wire loop on the turn signal. Alston had looked around, as if he could see anything beyond the tiny ring of light, and whispered, "Keys." If he'd taken his own truck keys he wouldn't be here now. But that wasn't something he'd ever even thought he'd need to do. There were things a person couldn't foresee. Like the owner of this old truck. Who would ever come out of the heart of this swamp and steal his truck? One of those flickering, disappearing willowy-wisps?

The old vinyl of the seat had been sticky against his back in the wet heat of the swamp and the first key Alston tried had been the right one. He backed carefully out of the drive and instead of turning to follow Margie, Alston drove deeper into the swamp. He was going to Kitty Hawk. He wanted to see the sun come up out of the ocean and feel what it would have been like if Margie had stayed with him. And he wanted to see what was there by the ocean that had made the Wright brothers fly. Maybe he'd be able to take some of it back to Margie.

That had been another fool's errand, Alston thought now. The policeman had stopped him for stealing the truck just before he reached Kitty Hawk, just before the sun was going to come out of the sea.

The policeman was beginning to turn a lot of corners and Alston knew they must be getting close. "I was going to take the truck back," Alston said. "She left me in the swamp."

"Must have been pretty rough for you," the policeman said

in a voice Alston hadn't heard before. He sounded as if he hated him.

"I rang their bell," Alston said. "Check for fingerprints if you want. I was just looking for help. I couldn't stay in that swamp all night. Not by myself. I borrowed that truck more than anything. I just couldn't stay there with those willowy-wisps."

The policeman didn't say anything. He was busy parking in a line of squad cars behind a large concrete building. When he took Alston out of the car he was rougher than he needed to be, and when he had Alston walking straight to the building he said, "That truck is the least of your problems, boy."

Alston looked over at the policeman who had a tight grip on his arm. The short hard bill of his hat was glossy black. "What do you mean?" Alston asked.

The policeman didn't answer. He went through the doors and nodded at another uniformed man behind a counter. "Rape," the policeman said. "And auto."

The other man took out some forms and the policeman undid Alston's handcuffs. The cuffs cut at his wrists but all Alston could feel was the word *rape*.

He remembered the angry screech of the tires and the engine dying and starting again, the red taillights fading away, leaving him without a chance. He thought of everything they'd done together in his truck, something he thought he'd remember forever, but already he wasn't clear exactly how things had happened, how that word could have possibly come up.

For an instant Alston tried to recall all he'd said in the squad car, when the policeman had seemed friendly; tried to remember every word that had left his mouth, tried to gauge his trouble, tried to find some way out. But instead his mind filled with Margie's face, like a freshly broken stone, showing all sharp, shiny angles, where before it had been smooth and rounded and familiar. He couldn't believe she'd become his enemy. He couldn't start thinking of her that way now. Not that fast.

Instead, he pictured Margie pulling into her driveway in his truck at five A.M., maybe crying again, her parents awake, their made-up overnight schedule falling apart, her father redder and louder every second, shouting that word into the phone to the police.

The new officer told Alston to empty his pockets on the counter and Alston stood motionless. The officer asked him again, and Alston turned to his policeman.

"Have you ever been to Kitty Hawk?" he whispered.

The policeman turned and looked at Alston. "Empty the pockets," he said. "Turn 'em out."

Alston started to fumble in his jeans. "Have you ever been to Kitty Hawk?" he asked again, remembering again how Margie had last said his name, the pleading tone, only now wondering what it was she had been begging him to do, or not do.

The policeman flipped his hand over and over, wanting Alston's pockets emptied. "Yeah, sure. Everybody's been there."

Alston put his wallet on the counter. "What's there?" he asked.

"There? Nothing but some dunes and stuff. Just the ocean."

Alston thought of the nauseating, slick swells, pushing up and falling down, over and over forever, and the flat line at the edge, which was really just more swells. "That's all?" he asked one more time. "That's it? Just the ocean?"

"There's some marker there—about the flight," the policeman said, looking at Alston again. "Why? What's so important about Kitty Hawk?"

"What kind of marker?"

"Just some concrete pillar. Why do you got to know about that?"

Alston grimaced and shook his head. Concrete. Like Margie's face. As if that would've shown them how to fly.

Cowbird

Finishing the last window I stepped back for a look, the reek of lead-free paint almost visible, like a fog. Still wrapped in wonder at the very idea of a baby here, I stood so long the brush dangling in my hand turned gummy, until Sybil's touch, coming from nowhere, nearly stopped my heart.

I leapt away, spinning around, my brush poised before me like a dagger. Then, grinning, but with my breath racing, I said, "Must be the paint."

Sybil whispered, "Sorry," but she looked only at the gleaming, empty room, not at me—my idiot's grin, my brandished weapon.

"Can you believe it?" she said in the same hushed voice, as if talking too loudly might let something hear, as if this were something it was still possible to jinx.

I shook my head and she wound her paint-stained fingers through mine, leaning to touch the side of her head against my shoulder. There was paint in her hair, too, tiny eggshell traces among the rare grays scattering the black gloss. "Once he's really here," I said.

After all the years of trying, I didn't need to finish. There'd been joking at first—the fun's in the trying—then years of seriousness: ovulation schedules, calendars and counting, body temperatures. The years of despair followed: sharing a bed but no more, a touch the wrong way bringing tears, not warmth. Finally there'd been Sybil's operation, opening things up, creating a better channel. It was farther than I wanted to go, but by then I was worried about her, afraid to deny anything she thought might be a chance.

After the surgery there were more years of trying, the returning loss of hope. It was Sybil who finally broached the subject of adoption. "It's something we should have been talking about for years," she insisted, catching my glance to the floor.

Of course we'd come close to discussing it before, but the whole idea made me queasy. Before getting my business degree, I'd started in biology—some last surge of high school enthusiasm over the tidy systems of nature, my amazement at opening that first frog; the identical layout of our insides, the tiny red jewel of the heart.

So I know science. I know genetics. I know about the different tactics employed to ensure a species' genes survive. I know about the cowbird, who lays its eggs in other, smaller birds' nests, lets those parents expend their energy passing on the cowbird's genes while the parents' own die with them. In that tidy system the young cowbird hatches first and rolls the real eggs out of the nest; kills whatever hatches from the eggs it cannot eject, or just out-eats them, starving the true offspring. Ensuring its own survival.

Of course I didn't say anything like that to Sybil. I only

said, "I don't know, Sybil. How do we know it'd be the same as having our very own?"

"It would be our baby, Tim," she answered.

"Maybe," I started, but backed off when I saw how disappointed in me she looked. "How can you always be so sure of everything?" I wondered out loud.

"All I'm sure of is how we'll feel if we don't ever have a child."

"Well, yes," I said. "That has become pretty clear." Sybil looked even more surprised than I felt hearing myself say such a thing, and that was as far as we got on adoption.

Until, at least a year after my blunder, Sybil again managed to weave the word into a conversation. It had the added connotation now of my ugly remark, and when I again glanced away, Sybil insisted. "Tim!"

She stared me down until I had to look back. "You can't say you haven't at least considered it?"

"Of course I have," I said, blowing out a sigh. "And I've read things, too."

"And?"

"And have some crack addict show up at our door five years from now, demanding her baby back? I don't think we need that, too, Sybil. On top of everything."

But, to my surprise, Sybil just waved her hand as if brushing away something ridiculous. "You'd be too careful for that, Tim. You know you would."

Her eyes shone. "I've been doing my own research, Tim. The Bosnian children, the orphaned refugees. The wait is half what it usually is. Less than half. We could—"

"Think, Sybil!" I blurted. "And wind up with some malnourished kid screaming in Serb in the middle of the night? Trying to take cover behind his bed, rocket fire searing his dreams?"

Sybil stared. I saw she actually had some literature in her hand. Some official watermark at its head. She'd been reaching it out toward me, but now she let her hand drop into her lap. "What have you become?" she asked.

I rubbed my face. "I'm sorry, Sybil. I didn't mean that. It's just so . . . so out of our control. So—"

"So much our only chance."

I stopped trying to say anything. Instead I forced a tiny smile and leaned forward to take the papers out of her lap. "Let's see," I said, my throat dry and scratchy.

Just the way Sybil had rolled out that, "You'd be too careful," started me thinking. She was right, of course. She knew me. So I started looking into things, checking every possible twist. I didn't start at the desperation end either; not with the war-torn Bosnians, the millions of abandoned Chinese girls. I started right here, in the state, and once I was certain we'd have no horror story about our baby being stolen away in the future, I finally talked to Sybil. The smile that flashed across her face made me ashamed I'd shied away so long.

So we went to an agency at last, looked into histories and wrote out our own. On their forms we invented our perfect child: a white newborn, free of defect. Then our second choice, where we'd be willing to compromise. Race, we decided, was not so important, and sex, of course, made no difference at all. We would accept a child up to one year old, but beyond that, I insisted, we'd be trying to fix other people's mistakes. Even if we weren't, there'd be so much we wouldn't know, so much out of our control. I would not even consider checking the box for special needs children, and I think Sybil was glad to have me say so, making the decision something she wouldn't have to torture herself over.

I thought of the saints of this earth who actually would check such a box, and though it was an odd feeling, admitting to myself that I was not now, and never would be, numbered among them, in the back of my mind, so far back I can't truly say I thought it even to myself, was the idea that all this paperwork was merely going through the motions. I'd heard so many stories about other people adopting. "They tried for years, and sure enough, two days after they adopt, she's pregnant." "Adopted their first, next year twins of their own." It took the pressure off, people said. Let natural processes unfold. It gave me hope.

But one year stretched to three and waiting for word of an adoptable baby began to loom as darkly as waiting for that first missed period had. Still did, in my case. I never gave up expecting Sybil to walk out of the bathroom some morning, a shy, almost terrified smile on her face. I knew exactly how she'd look at the floor, then me, then the floor again, finally whispering, "I'm late." Maybe even pulling one of the home tests from behind her back, showing me the little pink spot, our baby's first mark in the world. Hatching first, growing strong before the cowbird could land.

And then, when the call came at last, *We have very good news,* we only had two weeks to prepare. Envisioning an empty, dusty nursery growing old with us, I hadn't let Sybil start anything until we were sure. So we scrambled to buy the crib, the changing table, the bassinet; the diapers, toys, and blankets. Sybil blossomed, smiling at every purchase, sorting through them again and again. Every day it seemed she brought something new into the house, bright boxes stacking up in the living room while I did the dirty work of gutting the spare bedroom, rebuilding it as the nursery; both of us finally working side by side to finish the painting in time.

So, we stood in that remodeled bedroom a long time, Sybil

and I, knowing that at the other end of the state a baby was about to be born; the mother a strong, healthy, seventeen-year-old, a good kid, not into drugs, carrying good grades even through this. Just a bad decision, a mistake. The father, too; a steady kid, honor student even, something of a track star, impossible to find fault in. We hadn't had to settle for second choices, for compromises. On paper, these were kids you'd be proud to be parents of. This was almost like inheriting a grandchild.

We'd pick the baby up the first day. We could meet the girl for a moment if she wanted that, and if Sybil did; otherwise we'd deal only with the woman from the agency. The baby was a boy, we knew, having paid for every possible test. "You'd be too careful," Sybil had said, and she was right.

"Do you still like Ryan?" Sybil asked, squeezing my fingers in the empty, ready nursery.

"Ryan," I said, imagining the countless times I'd say it over the course of my life, a name now as important as Sybil's.

"It was my father's name," she whispered.

I smiled. "I know, Sybil," I answered, stepping away to drop my brush into the thinner can. I pushed open the windows, letting the room air, hoping the paint had filmed enough not to pick up every bit of dust, every passing bug. "Stop worrying, Sybil. Ryan is ours."

And, four days before the due date, he was. As we were led to the nursery, before we'd even seen the baby, Sybil asked if she could meet the mother. I began to advise against it, but Sybil turned, stopping me with a smile. "Shush, you," she said.

I gave in. We were so close now, and really, this was her dream coming true.

So, I followed her into the delivery room, the nurses still cleaning up afterward. A curved stainless-steel pan held a lot of blood, and it was a moment before I could look beyond that. When I did, I saw a pretty, pale girl, her hair sweat-flattened around her face, scattered in strings across the pillow. I was surprised to see the father there, a lean stretch of boy standing tight beside the bed, as pale and worn as the mother, still holding her hand. I nodded to him, trying not to smile, but glad about the evident character the baby would inherit.

The girl's lip slipped from between her teeth and her chin trembled. She said something. "Take care of him, please. Of Jason," though I'm not really sure that was it. She was already starting to cry, and the boy hovered over her, petting her forehead, whispering things. I took Sybil's arm. This was between the two of them, something nobody should be watching.

Sybil let herself be led from the room, whispering, "Thank you, thank you," until we were again in the hallway, stumbling toward the nursery.

We saw him through the glass first, a tag at the end of his clear plastic bassinet only saying, "Huntford Boy." No Jason about it. No Ryan.

His face was tiny, closed, red, the blankets surrounding him starkly white. Sybil let me hold more of her weight as she said, "That's him. That's our boy."

"Ryan," I said. I was grinning. I couldn't help it.

But when the nurse let us in, let us pick Ryan up, the first thing Sybil said, even as she rearranged her arms, cradling his head, was, "We shouldn't let them do this, Tim. They can't know how hard it will be."

"Sybil," I started, no idea what to say next, though I'd been afraid of just this all day. Sybil, unlike me, could easily be counted among those saints here on earth.

But the agency woman came to the rescue, quietly

soothing, telling us how all adoptive parents felt that way, but that the decision, by both couples, had been struggled over and reached correctly, how agonizing over it now was just that— agonizing.

Sybil let herself be calmed, but then, on our way out of the hospital, as she carried the tiny, silent bundle, everything signed and fail-safe, Ryan opened his eyes—deep, dark irises gazing up at us for the first time—and Sybil broke down. She cried so hard I had to take Ryan from her while she wiped her eyes, clinging to my arm.

"We can't take him from her, Tim. We just can't."

Though I wanted to stop, wrap an arm around her, I didn't risk it, and I kept pushing for the door. I was afraid Sybil would stagger back around, talk the mother into keeping her baby, warning her of all that could lie ahead. I held Ryan in the arm away from Sybil, safe there, and I stumbled all of us along, repeating the agency woman's speech about agonizing as if it were some sort of mantra.

By the time we reached the doors, the sun, and had wrestled Ryan's car seat under the belt in back, Sybil stopped snuffling. In fact, tears still streaming down her face, she couldn't stop smiling. Ryan was already asleep again, his tiny red face scrunched up inside the nearly solid wrap of blankets, and for a long minute we stayed bent over in the car, one of us on each side, just watching.

When we finally stood, straightening our backs, we looked over the roof of the car at each other. I smiled, tapping the roof once for luck. "So," I said, letting out a rush of pent-up breath. "Off we go."

Sybil bit her lip, nodding, smiling so hard I thought she might cry again. "Do you mind?" she asked, and before she gave a frail wave toward the back I was already shaking my head.

Cowbird

"Go ahead," I said. "He'll need you back there."

We drove all the way home that way, me alone in front, Sybil whispering progress reports from the back: "He turned his head." "He opened his hand." "Oh, Tim, he yawned."

The crying didn't begin until we were safely home, which I took to be a good omen. There we had all the equipment we'd bought and surrounded ourselves with, as if it might seep knowledge. We changed him, smiling at all the loose wrinkles of skin, fumbling as we taped up the tiny diaper. "Are we doing this right?" Sybil asked, and we both laughed, knowing the answer was that we didn't know. We didn't know a thing.

As we worked, Ryan weakly flailed his arms, and every touch of his tiny, bendy fingers against my wrist, my palm—accidental though they were—was an electric touch between our hearts. I was embarrassed I'd ever thought he'd seem alien to our lives.

Bouts of crying broke the long stretches of his sleep, filling our house with a sense of purpose that had never existed before. We found ourselves waiting for them, the changing table filled, the next batch of formula already mixed and cooled, a single bottle kept warm, ready at the first whimpering call.

Change him, feed him, burp him. It was all there was to do. Gas became our only enemy. I walked Ryan around the house at night, tapping gently on the back smaller than my hand, his oversized squalls tight against my ear. Sybil walked beside me every minute of it, whispering, "You're all right, my big strong boy. You're all right. You're just growing so fast already. It's only growing pains."

Her voice had such a sweetness, such sincerity even whispering nonsense, that I couldn't help but wonder that this had happened to me. Feeling her words brushing over both of us, Ryan's racing heartbeats like a tiny overwound toy against my chest, I knew, for the first time, the work of God.

We fumbled through our inexperience bit by bit and Ryan sailed through his two-week check-up, Sybil and I unable to think of any real complaints. Finally I said, "He seems to cry a lot," but Sybil and I both laughed immediately, saying, "Not that we have any idea how much is normal."

The doctor smiled with us. She said that's the only way he has to communicate. "Pretty soon he'll smile," she said. "Then you'll forget he ever cried."

We told her how he'd begun to focus on us, track our movements with his eyes. I knew we sounded as if we thought we were the only people this had ever happened to, but I couldn't stop telling her, couldn't hide my amazement.

As we said thank you and good-bye, the doctor actually hugged each of us, telling us how happy she was for our whole family.

It wasn't until a few weeks after that visit that the bouts of crying began to grow truly alarming.

Then, his face gone nearly purple, eyes squeezed tightly shut, or opened wide in such an expression of disbelief, his mouth stretched in helpless pain, we'd rock him and pat him, the formula he would not take dribbling over his lips, his new dry diaper immaculately white against the straining flush of his body. Sybil and I would pass him back and forth, sometimes holding him together, Sybil's whispery assurances taking on a tone as desperate as the expression on Ryan's face.

When Sybil held him without me I'd sit beside her and sweat, soaking through shirt after shirt. When I held him, she chewed her lip raw, tears trickling down her cheeks.

Finally he cried so hard that he suddenly went silent, his arms drawn up to his chest, trembling, his mouth yawing, eyes rolling toward the top of his head. Sybil cried, "Tim!" and I took him. As if by magic, he restarted, but within a few days he did it again. And again.

The doctor recommended a particular brand of drops for gas, but assured us this was normal, his digestive tract getting the hang of things. There'd be gas and it would be uncomfortable and he would cry. The drops, I had a feeling, were little more than a placebo for the parents.

I told her we knew about gas, he'd had gas, but this was not that, this was something more. I described what I called his convulsions, but she said he was only sucking in a big breath, that he had to, to cry. She soothed us, her tone something completely different from Sybil's, something professional, a way she talked every day to the endless line of overwrought parents. We took Ryan home and pumped him full of drops, collapsing onto the couch when he finally slept, more exhausted than from any work or exercise we'd ever done.

Sybil was the first to raise the word *colic*. We'd joked past our fears of it while we finished his nursery, turning over the horror stories we'd heard: four-hour bouts of inconsolable crying; driving round and round the city, praying for the motion and white noise of the road to bring sleep.

It seemed so funny now, so pathetic, that our worries had been only for ourselves.

The doctor, when we called, told us every new parent cried *Colic!* at the first long stretch of crying. Colic doesn't usually appear, she said, until the sixth week, though our books put it at the second or third. It was all perfectly normal, she said again, making me finally shout, "Come over here and hold him while he screams! Feel him twist tight as a knot! Then you tell me about normal!"

Sybil took the phone from me without a word, began

talking to the doctor with her own soothing tone, arched with just a bit of steel. We took him back in the next week, and got a prescription. More drops.

"Perfectly normal, my ass," I said as we drove home from the pharmacy, Ryan winding up again in his car seat, Sybil trying to put in a pacifier.

Falling back to genetics, I was tempted to call the parents of the girl, the mother, and ask what she'd been like as a baby, what her brothers and sisters had been like. But our contact with them had been cut, forever and permanently, and everything I read made no mention of a genetic link for colic.

So we endured until finally, after talking Sybil into going out shopping alone, a break from the heartrending shouts, I slipped down to the doctor's office with Ryan, determined not to leave until something had been done.

I walked past the receptionist without a word, nothing but Ryan's squalling, and found the doctor just lifting a manila folder out of the bracket in front of a door, some other person's child waiting inside, not my concern.

"Listen!" I demanded, and as I held Ryan toward her he went silent, back arched, trembling arms drawn in, eyes rolling. Resisting the urge to pull him back, to go through all my futile efforts at comforting him, I held him out there alone in the air.

With a quick glance at the receptionist, who, without my knowing, had trailed me down the hallway, the doctor held out her hands for Ryan. I gave him to her, guiltily happy to be rid of him for just that instant, to give him up to more experienced hands, more knowledgeable care.

That's when the tests began in earnest. Batteries of tests. I spent hours holding Ryan as he screamed, crying myself finally as he clutched at me, so scared, asking only for protection while I clamped him down so they could plunge in another needle, take yet more of his blood. His eyes, only focusing for weeks, never left mine, brimming over with tears as his mouth formed a tiny frown, his lower lip quaking.

Eventually they needed him alone, needed to put him under, and I gave him over feeling as if I might throw up, my legs unsteady as I walked alone to the waiting room to sign the paperwork, vaguely guilty at the shadow of relief I felt at no longer having to hold him, having to watch his trust while I stood so helpless.

As I fiddled with toys meant for toddlers, watching the receptionist make the calls canceling the day's appointments, I began to hope there really was something they could find, find and fix. Yet, at the same time, I tried to prepare myself, to at least acknowledge that there might be something terribly wrong, that no one could ever fix. I know I did not once think of the adoption contract, the various legal clauses.

Eventually I was sent home, without Ryan. I'd called Sybil, assured her everything was fine, not to come down, but when I pulled into the driveway with that empty car seat, she met me at the car door, demanding that we return to the doctor's, that we couldn't leave Ryan alone and frightened there.

I got out as quickly as I could, reaching Sybil before she could get in and buckle herself down. "Sybil," I said, holding her. "Sybil, it's all right. Being there doesn't do any good. We can't even see him right now."

I held her, a hand on each shoulder. "They're finally taking us seriously, Sybil. They're finally going to get to the bottom of this."

"He's just colicky," Sybil said, going limp, her forehead resting against my chest, her words hardly more than a whimper, colic suddenly something to hope for.

The doctor's call, when it came later that afternoon, was cool and concerned, but after she hung up, I had a feeling it had also been laced with an undertone of apology. Something found now that perhaps should have been found earlier. I hung up slowly, looking at the receiver.

Beside me, Sybil pleaded, "Tim? What?"

"They're going to keep him overnight at the hospital."

"Why?" Sybil's voice rose like the rocket fire I'd imagined for our Bosnian child.

"Only more tests," I said, still staring at the phone, but reaching an arm around her shoulders. "Only more tests."

"I'm getting together a bag," Sybil said, steely again. "I will not spend a night here without him. He will not spend a night alone, without me. He will not wake up without me."

"I'll start the car," I answered.

Those tests, and the specialists with their additional tests, took Ryan quickly past colic. Soon we were seated around a conference table, surrounded by doctors and the soft glow of a light board covered with pictures of Ryan's head: X rays and CTs, MRIs—all of them—a ghostly black-and-white collage.

The doctors spelled out the problem, their inability in the face of it. They talked, their voices only a blur around Sybil and me, the two of us holding on to each other, withdrawing into ourselves in our chairs.

Complete failure to develop mentally, they said, going on in hard scientific terms that once would have interested me, but all I heard now was blindness, deafness, lifelong intensive care. The kind of care required was, they said, practical only in an institution.

Sybil was crying out loud. I held her so tightly I worried I might hurt her. And I looked up, looked at all those educated faces almost looking back at me. Over their shoulders glowed the bright pictures of Ryan's defective brain.

"Was this something we could have known about before?" I asked. "That anyone could have known about already?"

They shook their heads together, as if all controlled by the same puppeteer. "With an apparently normal infant, there'd be no reason to look," they said. "Until this age, everything appears normal."

"Completely?" I pressed. "Even with all our tests? The ultrasounds?"

"Those wouldn't show this. That's not their intention."

"I have a contract," I said, getting to my feet, my voice trembling. "A legal contract. It says this baby will be healthy."

I felt Sybil tug at my arm, trying to pull me back down with her. I saw the doctors look at the table.

"It guarantees this baby's health!" I shouted, jerking my sleeve away from Sybil's grasp.

"And?" said one of the doctors, a specialist whose name I could not recall. He looked up at me. "And if he's not?"

"The contract is null. We do not have to accept this child!"

The room was silent after my shouts and, after standing there shaking a moment, I turned to leave, to follow Sybil, to find her wherever she'd run while I'd shouted.

I caught up to her in another waiting room, an empty chapel of some sort. "Sybil," I said. "Sybil."

She turned away from me, arms wrapped tight around herself, shrugging her shoulder out from under my hand.

"I didn't mean anything," I whispered. "Sybil. I was shouting nonsense. I can't even think, Sybil."

Slowly she looked up at me, as if I were a species she had not encountered before. "What about Ryan?" she said. "What are we going to do, Tim?"

"The very best we can," I answered, and this time when I reached for her she allowed me back into her arms.

But after another night watching Ryan twist and squall,

leaning our heads against the hospital crib's cool stainless side-bars when he finally slept, our tears striking the hard waxed linoleum, Sybil and I sat wrung-out, barely able to speak, let alone think.

"Sybil," I whispered at last, really whispered, doing everything possible to keep Ryan from waking. "We can't live through this," I said. "This will kill us."

Ryan's breaths, so calm and quiet, filled the air between us.

"It will be the hardest thing we've ever done," Sybil answered.

We'd never done anything hard, I realized. Not once. All the years that a baby became only something we lost hope in—the worst thing that had ever happened to us—were nothing.

"We can't do it," I said.

Sybil put her hand across my shoulders. "We can," she said. "If we have to."

I looked at Ryan, just a sleeping baby, his chest rising and falling beneath the blankets. Sleeping with his mouth open, a funny triangle-shaped hole that had always come so close to breaking my heart.

"We don't have to," I murmured. "Sybil, we don't. The contract . . ."

Sybil's arm jerked from my back. The movement, too quick, too alarming, made me flinch, made me glance to Ryan, praying she hadn't woken him.

"The agency, Sybil," I said. "They're equipped to handle this kind of thing. We aren't. We never could be."

Sybil rocked in her chair, letting the silence stretch out and out. Finally she whispered, "Remember when we started this? Filling out our perfect-baby forms? How on the way home you marveled at discovering that you were not a saint?"

"Sybil."

"That was not a revelation for me, Tim. That was not even a surprise."

I gave her a minute, then said only, "Think."

At home, when we finally talked again, both of us sitting on the edge of the bed, knowing we wouldn't sleep, putting off even undressing, I said, "Sybil? We didn't bargain on this. We wanted a child, Sybil. One who will grow up, who will go to school, who will play games. One we can teach to walk and talk. Who'll laugh with us. Do we want to tie our lives down now?"

I took a breath. "Sybil?" I said, though she'd given no sign she was even capable of hearing me. "Sybil," I said again. "We can get another, Sybil. It's in the contract. We don't even lose our place in the list. We're still on top."

"On top?" she asked, without an indication that she wasn't the only living thing on the planet. "To start this over?"

I thought of the empty nursery, of it growing old and dusty with us, the storms driving the rain under the windows, the paint on the sills lifting and bubbling over the years, drying and cracking. "Yes," I said.

"Just take Ryan back?"

"It's not something we should have to do," I said, meaning even being faced with such a decision, having to make such an inhuman choice.

But Sybil said, "So, because this isn't the game we wanted to play, we can just quit? Return the faulty piece?"

"Just think, Sybil," I whispered. "Just think." And I held my head, giving us both time to think, though I knew it was something we'd be doing for the rest of our lives. I watched Sybil hugging herself tight, rocking back and forth.

"Visiting him in some hospital, Sybil," I said at last. "Waiting for him to give up." I was crying myself now, though Sybil was dry-eyed. "That's not something we can do, Sybil." I meant to say that it wasn't something she could do, that I worried about her health, her mind, going through something so horribly wrong after all this, but it didn't come out that way.

"Don't you see what giving him up would do to you, Tim? To us? Can't you see even that? How far beyond whatever damage keeping him could do?"

"Sybil," I whispered. "It's impossible, I know."

She turned to look at me, a hope filling her eyes, as if I could now explain things, could make things better, after I thought she was growing to hate me while I'd sat there talking.

"The cowbird, Sybil," I said. I saw confusion tatter her hope, but I went on. "Do you think the other birds, the hosts, do you think that if they knew, that if somehow they saw what had been done to them, that they'd just let it happen?"

"Tim?" she said.

"Do you think for one second they'd keep that big, strange egg in their nest? It's going to destroy them, for God's sake! It's going to kill their own babies! It's going to bleed them dry making them care for it. They'll never ever raise their own young. A cowbird! Not even their own kind!"

"Tim!" Sybil snapped, as if I'd gone hysterical, lost in a tirade I could be shocked out of. "Tim, you're not making sense. What are you talking about?"

"Sybil," I started, "that's how—"

But Sybil leapt up, shouting, "That's how you see Ryan? Some kind of parasite?" She glared at me a moment more, then charged into the bathroom, actually locking herself in.

I couldn't help but think of her last pregnancy test, still boxed beneath the sink.

I stood outside the door, whispering, "Sybil," but eventually sat back down on the end of our bed, staring at myself in the big mirror over the dresser.

I wondered if I was evil, flawed in some way I'd never suspected. Or was I, as she once thought, only careful, only weighing options? I thought of Ryan fighting for everything in the burnished steel crib across town, wondered how I could ever let him go.

The cowbird, like most birds, is born with a sharp, hard beak, which it uses to break its way out of its shell. It's also what it uses to work under the other eggs, the ones not yet hatched, starting them on their way out of the nest, on their long, long fall.

The people from the agency came early in the day, and we met them at the hospital. Mercifully, Ryan was asleep and peaceful. He clutched Sybil's finger when she touched his palm, and I turned away, hiding my own hands deep in my pockets.

At home that evening Sybil again startled me in the nursery. I was shutting the windows tight, locking them, trying to keep the rain from blowing in, when she said, "Tim?"

Instead of jumping this time, I froze, hands on the cold window glass, thin bands of condensation outlining my hand-prints for an instant when I took them away. It could be a game I'd show our children someday. I was sweating the way I had when we could not stop or understand Ryan's screaming.

"I'm sorry," she said.

I shrugged, and we stood apart in the crowded, silent room.

"He's not a cowbird," I answered, but we hadn't talked

much recently, and my voice was scratchy and cracked. "I never meant that."

She touched my back, her hands against my shoulder blades, softly. "Of course," she whispered.

If she only changed the force of her touch, I thought, I'd be sailing now, straight through the locked window, out into the storms.

"I just never expected to miss him so," I said, thinking that he had never said a word, never smiled, never done anything but sleep or cry, yet he had become a part of life bigger even than myself.

I gazed out at the cold yard, the bare branches, Sybil behind me, just barely able to touch me.

When the big, drab cowbird finally fledged, I wondered, did the finches or warblers—the tiny, exhausted hosts—stand so stunned in their nests, knowing their time had passed?

Gluttony

"Yeah, she can cook," my boss, Matt, said to the plumbers. "She's a great cook. Big deal. Don't you get it? That's half the problem."

Even those of us who'd heard it before looked up from our lunches when he dumped his cooler onto the subflooring. Tupperware containers scattered across the rough plywood and Matt kicked at one. Stuffing and gravy spiraled out in long, slippery arcs.

"Ninety goddamn degrees and she cooks all day! Look at this! An entire Thanksgiving dinner!" He bent down searching through the containers he'd scattered. As he opened them he crowed, "Mashed potatoes! Creamed corn! Ah, look at this! Cranberry sauce! Can you believe it? In August?"

I looked down at the sandwich Mom made for me every morning, even now, months after high school. A single slice of bologna, some browning lettuce.

Rory, Matt's head carpenter, had told us that though Matt

was only forty, Nancy was his third wife, each one younger than the last. Nancy was twenty-eight, Rory said. He guessed number four might be a teenager. Rory hadn't been around for the first, but he said the second had gone just like this. Rages over nothing. Rory said Matt would be pretty tough to be around until his divorce, which he bet would be before the end of the summer. But number four would come along soon enough, Rory said, and we'd be on Easy Street for at least a year after that.

Just thinking of Nancy divorced, free, made me loose on the insides.

But the plumbers were new on the job and hadn't heard any of that history. They stared at Matt. "You're bitching about a lunch like that?" one of them asked.

Matt snatched his napkin off the floor, holding it up like a signboard. "How about this?" Written across the yellow paper in a girl's big, loopy handwriting was, "I love you!" in green ink. Just under that, in blue, was a huge, round smiley face. "God!" Matt said. "It's pathetic."

We all stared at him and Matt said, "Makes me sick," before stalking off to a window. He flicked at the slight roll pushing at the waist of his T-shirt, muttering, "She knows I'm trying to lose this weight." He tore an Anderson sticker off the glass, but the glue stuck fast and he couldn't see any better.

He picked at the glue with his thumbnail. "Dean," he said to me, "get a razor blade and get rid of these damn stickers."

I said, "You got it," starting to jump, but he told me to finish my sandwich first.

Later, when I was done with the windows, I cleaned up Matt's lunch, dumping it on the scrap pile growing alongside the house. I plucked the napkin out of the air as it fluttered down, before it could touch the broken bits of lumber and PVC, the scraps of Tyvek and flashing.

Gluttony

Glancing back toward the house, I stayed crouched over the junk, reading Nancy's message again. "I love you!"

The house we were building sat all alone on the side of a mountain, surrounded by huge old ponderosa pines. Some rich guy's place. As the job went on, I rode my bike up earlier and earlier, leaving coffee on for when Mom woke up. I'd be sweating and blowing by the time I leaned my bike against the retaining wall, but then it would be still and cool, the deep layers of long needles spongy beneath my boots, the trees sharp-smelling. I'd listen to them rustle in the quiet before anyone else came up and ruined it.

This was my first real job, and though I was only a laborer I considered it my apprenticeship. Sometimes I'd go through the whole house, picturing every step that had made each room, trying to see if I could remember when there was nothing here but a gash on the side of the hill, long before the scrap pile started to grow. I tried to catalog all the work in my head, trying to learn something, but I always wound up picturing those rooms in the future, filled with people who wanted to live here—moms and dads and kids—people who wanted to stay together in this house, the big whispering trees towering around them like some kind of impregnable fort.

I made up whole happy lives, people I would have recognized on the street. It got to where I even tried picturing me and Mom up here, happy and safe, maybe even with Dad back. Then I thought of just me and Nancy here, and after that I never thought of it any other way. I saw us chasing each other through the house, laughing, doing it in every room. Maybe we'd even have some kids of our own someday.

The only thing Matt ever said about the trees, of course,

was how leaving them so close to the house made everything more of a bitch. Throwing out lunch after lunch, he predicted how the trees would blow down, wrecking the house, squashing the rich guy or, if he was lucky, just his wife. He'd go on and on—background noise—and I'd stare at those tall, quiet trees, knowing at my house they'd stand forever.

The trash pile kept growing and every day when I dumped Matt's lunch I would see parts of others; some cake with white icing the wasps liked, a slab of roast beef thick with flies. Matt kept saying we were going to have to torch it soon, because of the stink, but whenever I asked if he wanted me to light it, he'd just glance out at the pile and shake his head.

During lunch Matt drank Diet Cokes while the rest of us ate. Used to be he'd talk hunting and fishing, long stories about all the times he'd nearly killed himself. He'd get us laughing so we could hardly eat. But now it was always about women, a lot about his first wife, how he'd just walked in one night and told her to pack her stuff. She'd stolen his rifle on the way out, he told everyone, but even so he was smiling, remembering himself telling her exactly where to get off.

A roofer told about coming home from an out-of-town job to find his house empty. "Carpets, fixtures. I mean everything. Gone. Got a letter about a month later with the address for child support."

One of the plumbers said he still saw his ex all the time, said they were pretty friendly. She even let the child support slide for a month or two if work was slow.

I looked at the plumber. "My mom still talks to my dad sometimes," I said. "Sometimes he stays over for dinner."

Everybody went quiet, looking at me, waiting for me to go on. I looked at the floor, feeling my face heat up. "When he comes to see me, I mean." I swallowed. "Just sometimes."

Matt stood up and checked his watch, shaking his head.

"No sense in that," he told the plumber and me. "Drop 'em like a bad habit. That's my motto."

I was on the roof sweeping off shingle scraps when Nancy came up to the site later that week, something she hardly ever did. As soon as I saw her little red Honda inching over the ruts, I crouched behind a dormer, watching her park, the quick bounce of her walk before she disappeared below the eaves.

Nancy did all the books for Matt, wrote all the checks, and after Mom and I had our knock-down drag-out about me not going to college, I saw Nancy every week. Mom made me pay rent after the fight and I got so far behind so fast I had to pick up my check as soon as Nancy signed it.

But even after I got my payments lined out I kept picking up my checks. I'd make a big deal about how broke I was and Nancy would smile and give me advice about finances. Seeing her hustling around in her shorts and tank top, smiling right at me, treating me like a real person, is how I started picturing the two of us together, up here in our house, miles from Matt. Of course, looking at her like that, I never heard a single word of whatever she was saying. It's not like I didn't know it was ridiculous. Even when I was only waiting for the divorce.

Lately I'd started going up to bed earlier and earlier, telling Mom work was wearing me out, feeling bad about lying to her. But then I'd lie sweating in the darkness, thinking about Nancy, as far from sleep as it was possible to get. And though I'd try to think of us as married, in love, the way parents are supposed to be, and though I knew I'd never, ever treat Nancy the way Matt did, I'd always end up picturing us in the dark, naked and sweaty and out of breath. I'd imagine all the things I thought Nancy could show me, things I'd only dreamed of, things that would take my breath away.

Nancy found Matt on the far side of the house putting up soffit and I stayed behind the dormer so I wouldn't have to see what happened. I could still hear it though, his "Goddamns," and, "How many times have I told you not to bother me on a job?"

The plumber who still liked his ex was up on the roof too, doing something with a vent stack. I glanced over at him, but he lowered his eyes, twisting at the piece of pipe.

In another minute Nancy walked back to her car and I slid around the dormer so I could watch without the plumber seeing. She had on a white shirt so thin I could see through to her bra strap, even from the top of the roof. Backing out, she twisted to look over her shoulder, her shirt pulling tight across her chest just as the glare off the windshield blinded me.

It wasn't fifteen minutes before Matt slammed his truck door and roared off down the side of the mountain. He wasn't back before we broke for lunch, and as we gathered in the shade of the living room the plumber who'd been on the roof asked, "What was that all about?"

Rory grinned, shaking his head. "He had a dentist appointment. She'd been calling all morning but he forgot to turn on the mobile."

We all chuckled, but the plumber said, "What the hell's she still mothering him for?"

"End of the summer," Rory predicted. "Not a minute more."

I swallowed hard. Maybe I had a chance. On the rebound.

"She seems smart enough," somebody said, and someone else added, "Not bad-looking."

The other plumber, the ugly one, grinned. "One tight piece of ass," he said.

Usually, any comment like that would lead into one of Matt's sex stories, but now everybody looked down at their scrawny lunches. Nobody said anything until I jumped up, grabbing Matt's cooler. "Hey!" I said. "Why don't we eat his?"

They all stared at me. "Come on," I said. "Save me the trouble of throwing it out."

The plumber with the nice ex stood up and together we peered into the cooler. Pretty soon everyone was there. We spread Matt's lunch out on the floor where the countertop would be. There was a mess of barbecued chicken wings and a huge square of lasagna. Rory popped the lid off a wedge of lemon cake that must have weighed half a pound. The whole kitchen smelled like an orchard.

"This is just the leftovers," the plumber said. "Imagine what he must get at home."

That's exactly what I was imagining, and I reached in first, pulling out a chicken wing and taking a bite. I imagined Nancy hot over the barbecue, turning her head away from the smoke, closing her eyes, her tongue poking out to wet her lips.

The others started to dig in too, and we laughed between bites, saying how if we had wives who looked like her, with the nerve to pack us lunches like this, we'd sure be divorcing them too. As we settled back to finish the cake the plumber I didn't like sighed and said, "I know I could stand a little of her mothering."

I hated him.

Then we heard Matt's truck, straining back up the mountain. We glanced around at each other. "What are we going to tell him?" Rory wanted to know.

The truck was getting close and I leapt up with the cooler, throwing all the empty containers back inside. I ran to the trash pile and began acting like I was scooping his lunch into all the other junked scraps.

Matt walked by me as if I wasn't there. But he nodded and said, "Couldn't eat if I wanted to. Can't even feel my face."

When he was safely past I pulled the napkin from the cooler. It was a flowered one today, Nancy's handwriting in bright red. I was winded from my rush to hide what we'd done and as I took slow, deep breaths I read, "I still love you!" *Still* was underlined three times.

I turned away from the trash in time to see Matt walking through the hole where the front door would go. Without wanting to, I pictured Nancy at home alone, cooking, writing notes to her husband on napkins. I wondered if Matt told her he threw it all out, that he was one day going to light a fire big enough to drive away the stench.

The Tupperwares bounced hollowly as I dropped them back into the cooler. I read the napkin one more time, then crumpled it, rubbing my hands over the words, making it look like Matt had used it, but ignored her anyway. Then I put the napkin in the cooler too, where Nancy would find it. She'd be so much better off without him.

The painters and the cabinet guys came up to the house pretty soon, and then the carpet layers, the job winding up fast. We had some commercial building downtown next that I wasn't looking forward to at all. A house you can at least pretend you're going to live in someday.

On what was going to be my last day, I got out of bed extra early. I had to Windex all the glass, a job I hate, but tomorrow I'd be downtown, oiling concrete forms, and I wanted to spend a last morning surrounded by those big trees. I tiptoed around our tiny house, making my own lunch and filling the coffee-maker for Mom. At the last second, thinking of her walking around as loud as she wanted, alone, I pulled a napkin from the holder and wrote, "Have a nice day!" The pen tore the paper and the note looked as stupid as anything I'd ever done, but I left it under her cup anyway.

I pedaled hard, my head down as I climbed the mountain, which is why I didn't notice the smoke until the last stretch. There was a thick, ropy plume of it roaring up from the trees and for an instant my heart nearly stopped. But even as I struggled for breath I realized it was only the scrap pile. Once the smoke reached the top of the trees it seemed to drift, not quite sure where to go once the burning heat died out.

I pumped the pedals even harder, thinking Matt had really gone over the edge, leaving a pile like that to burn all night with no one to watch it. But as I rode past his truck into the driveway I saw that the pile was just getting going, not something that had smoldered all night. I left my bike against the embankment and walked up to watch the fire.

Matt was squatted down over his heels, what he called gook-style, back just far enough to keep from getting burned, his face raw from the heat. He didn't bother looking at me when I came up beside him and I watched the fire rage a long time. I was beginning to think he didn't even know I was there when he said, "What are you doing here so early?"

I pictured the house I'd imagined over the months, me and Nancy inside. It was so early we wouldn't be dressed yet. Wouldn't even be out of bed, though we'd been awake for hours. "I come up early a lot," I said. "I like it here."

He wasn't listening.

"What are you doing up here?" I asked.

"Had to burn this pile," he said. "Should have done it a month ago."

"I would have," I said.

"I moved out last night," Matt answered, as if that explained why he hadn't let me start the fire. "Spent the night up here in that rich fucker's bedroom." He smiled into the flames. "How do you think he'd like that?"

Thinking of Matt spending a night in our bedroom, I stared at his back, hunched over Nancy's burning lunches. "He wouldn't care," I said. "He'll never even know."

For the first time since I'd ridden up Matt looked at me. "Dean," he said, "why don't you go into town? Give Rory a hand with the foundation. Hold the leveling rod or something."

"What about the windows?"

"Forget the goddamn windows!" he shouted. He looked back at the fire and took a deep, wavery breath. He flipped a broken bit of door trim into the flames. "Just go away."

I stepped backward until I reached my bike, not taking my eyes off of him, the last look Nancy or I'd have to have.

I didn't ride downtown. Instead I pedaled up Matt's street, surprised to see how normal everything looked. As I leaned my bike against the brick wall and took off my helmet, I caught a shiver of goose bumps wondering what I'd find inside.

When I got up my nerve, Nancy answered the bell before I got my finger off the button. But then she only stared at me a second before saying, "Oh. Dean. Payday already?"

I said, "Yep," though I knew she knew it wasn't payday.

She said, "Come on in," already walking toward the back of the house where she kept the books. She was wearing nothing but a tank top that was way too big for her. It was long enough it could have hidden shorts, but I realized that this was what she had slept in, alone last night, and that she hadn't even bothered getting dressed today.

When she came back Nancy was holding a check, but she said, "I'm sorry, Dean. I don't know what to make this for."

She really did seem sorry and I said, "Same as ever." I looked close at her. "Except not today, Nancy. I quit." I'd never said her name that way, right to her face.

"You quit?" she repeated.

"I couldn't work for him anymore, Nancy," I said, needing to let her know everything. "Not now."

She stared at me. I couldn't think of another thing to say.

Nancy set the blank check on the counter and looked all around her kitchen, as if suddenly surprised to find herself standing there. I couldn't tell if she was going to cry or smile. "Say, Dean," she said all of a sudden, "I was just going to cook a little breakfast. Could I fix something for you?"

I worked on keeping my breathing shallow, unable to believe this was going to come true.

She picked up a pair of eggs, palming them in one hand, showing them to me. "Just a little something?" she said.

When I managed to nod, she turned to the stove and still holding the eggs in one hand she broke them into a cold pan. She knifed a slab of butter in after the eggs and turned on the gas. Even I knew you didn't cook eggs that way.

But as she worked with the eggs I looked at her—at the whole side of her breast through the loose shoulder strap of her top, rising and falling with her breaths. She wasn't wearing a bra and her breast stood up almost as straight as I'd imagined.

I closed my eyes a second, trying to think of her the way I did at night, but this close I'd seen the thin, milky-blue veins climbing the side of her breast, and I only thought of how, before I started going up to the house so early, Mom and I ate breakfast like this together—how when I was little, Dad would be there, too, pouring me cereal. And though I wanted to stay here more than anything, I said, "My mom and I already ate, Nancy. I couldn't fit in another bite."

But I was staring at the side of her almost-perfect breast when Nancy turned, catching me red-handed.

The sizzle around the eggs grew loud and I turned away. "I got to go," I said.

"Where?" she asked. "Where is there to go?"

I grazed the door with the tips of my fingers. "I don't know," I said, thinking of Mom, who was probably waking up right now, finding the coffee I'd left for her, that pathetic note. Dad in his little apartment.

"Don't you need your check?" Nancy asked. She picked it up from the counter, holding it toward me still blank.

I moved toward her, but didn't lift my hand to take the check. I stopped close, closer than normal, close enough I could pretend I felt the warmth of her breath against my neck. I stared at her thin, naked legs, reliving all my nights, afraid to lift my eyes.

The eggs were beginning to scorch.

Taking a big breath, I whispered, "I, Nancy, we . . ."

But then, as if jolted awake by the smell of the eggs, Nancy spun away from me toward the stove. Instead of reaching for the pan, though, jerking it off the burner, she just stood and stared. She gave a tiny stamp of her bare foot, the sound of it against the linoleum a naked slap. "I can't even *cook* anymore," she said.

"Nancy," I answered, "I love your cooking."

Still without doing anything about the eggs, Nancy turned back to me. "What?"

"He always made me throw it out, but once I saved it all! We ate it, everything!" It all came out in a rush. "There were wings, and cake, and, and . . . It was the best, Nancy! The best I—"

I stopped, seeing Nancy leaning toward me, squinting, as if she couldn't see me, or remember who I was. She looked surprised, or even hurt maybe.

I stammered a second before blurting, "You're just so beautiful, Nancy!"

I reached past the check she still held, reached to touch her, maybe even pull her into me at last. I looked up to meet her eyes and I saw she was smiling, just barely, and I smiled too. "Nancy," I said, wondering if I could actually tell her I loved her, right now, face to face, the way I always did at night, sweat-slicked and breathless.

"Poor Dean," she said, her smile growing a little more steady. "How old are you?"

I lowered my hand. "Almost eighteen," I said. "But—"

Nancy reached to pat my arm. "Poor Dean," she said again.

Then, finally, she turned and plucked the pan off the stove. In one slick move she shoved it into the sink and knocked back the faucet. The cold water screamed and boiled against the hot pan, clouds of steam billowing up.

Only then did Nancy look back at me, shaking her head. "So," she said, taking a breath, leaning back against her counter, still smiling sadly, the way she had when she'd said *Poor Dean.*

I bumped backward into the door, throwing it open as soon as I could find the knob. I leapt down the steps, almost tripping as I flung my leg over the seat of my bike. From behind, I heard her calling my name, "Dean, wait. Dean!" But I pedaled away as hard as I could, breathing as if I'd just come up from too long under water. I fled, away from Nancy and all our empty, sweaty nights, only hoping that I could still catch Mom before she was gone.

Doors

I stare at my son's door. Getting through school, I worked for a carpenter, a gofer more than anything, but even so, you pick up some things. This door is a hollow core, built for privacy, not security. Two wafer-thin panels and some diagonal cardboard slats give it all the stiffness it'll ever have. Even if the stops held—the hinges and latch—I could shatter right through the veneer, tear apart the flimsy bracing.

But what then? I'd only land inside Robert's room. Before he was born, Darleen and I'd slept there ourselves. I know all I need to know about the room.

And in the last month or so, we've actually started seeing Robert again, sliding up the stairs, disappearing into his room; he and that girl finally allowing some air to slip between them. Darleen wondered if there was trouble but, not wanting to get my hopes up, I said, "Probably just coming up for breath."

Catching Robert once before he could close his door, I said, "Haven't seen much of Tonya lately."

He stopped, his hand on the knob, his back to me.

I gave him a second, then smiled, "I mean, it's almost like you live here again."

He turned to look at me, a surprised look of what could have almost passed for hatred. "Just happy to be here," he murmured, then closed the door between us, hard.

Walking away now, I can't keep back a shiver. That gaze of his. How a sixteen-year-old can make me feel so extraneous is beyond me. I mean, this is my own house, my own life.

I almost turn back to his room then, burst through his door without checking to see if he bothers locking it anymore. Give him a good solid cuffing. Just to make him acknowledge I'm still here. But Darleen and I have never struck him, knowing the battle lost with the first blow.

But, holding on to the railing at the top of the stairs, I'm ashamed how pleasing the image of that open-hand slap against his cheek is, his dumbfounded shock, his late surge of howling indignation.

Robert comes down for dinner, slouching into his chair without a word, as if disgusted at this weakness of his body, the need for something as ordinary as food forcing him into such close proximity to us.

"Hello, Robert," I say, though I know it bothers him. Because of that. "How was your day?"

Robert slides to the other side of his chair, peers past his eyebrows toward Darleen at the stove. He reaches for his fork though there is nothing in front of him. Not even a plate.

Darleen gives me a look.

"Lost my head," I say.

Robert sinks lower in his chair, though you wouldn't have thought that possible. He rolls his eyes.

"How was school?" I ask, unable to help myself.

He directs his brow-down gaze at me for a moment. "Super."

"Swell," I answer.

Darleen sets something between us on the table. It's a chicken, browned and steaming, cut into legs and wings, breasts and back. "There's rice," she says, handing out plates.

I turn my chair away from Robert, finished with him for another night. "I think we landed the state contract," I tell Darleen, what I've been wanting to say since I came home.

"Swell," Robert mutters.

I catch a trace of his smile, his pleasure at spitting that back my way.

"Yes," I answer, smiling back. "Looks as if you'll be able to lodge here a while longer after all."

"That's great," Darleen says, placing the rice and a dish of asparagus spears in their positions. "About the state."

Worrying about Robert with Darleen, I've brought up the idea of eviction. Not a plan at all, just brainstorming, searching for some way to make him recognize us again. But Darleen doesn't let even the idea go that far. It's a phase, she says, one we have to get through without losing him.

"It's a year's work," I say to Darleen, still barely daring to breathe the sigh of relief I've been holding all day.

"Keep your nose to the grindstone," Robert mutters.

"Idle hands; the devil's playground," I answer. We used to talk like that all the time.

Robert reaches for a drumstick.

As we eat, Darleen asks about the contract, and I give some details, Robert not bothering to interrupt with any of our old bromides sharpened to weapons. Dinners have grown into this; as if we're practicing for old age, just the two of us eating together, the ghost of Robert watching from his chair.

Finally I can't stand it anymore. Regardless of the price Darleen will exact later, I turn my chair to face Robert head-on across the table. "So," I say. "Enough about me. How have you been keeping yourself busy?"

He shrugs, chewing. His hair, vaguely oiled and finger-combed straight back, a style I haven't seen since the fifties, drops over his temples, swinging toward his eyes with every grinding chomp.

"What's been on your mind?" I ask, leaning back to watch him. "What plans do you have? What grand visions fill your future?"

Robert pushes his own chair back and stares at me.

"Now that you and Tonya aren't joined at the hip, how on earth do you manage to simply stand up?"

Robert swallows, for a second appearing almost nervous, but then sliding back into his mask of contempt.

"Just this evening," I begin, "I stood outside your door, picturing how easy it'd be to break through it. Straight into your room to slap that look off your dumb, smug face."

"Stop it!" Darleen says.

"So," I go on, "I got wondering what ideas *you've* been cooking up. What you've been up to since you quit speaking to us."

Robert just keeps staring at me, as if not a day passes without me telling him to expect a beating. But then he says, "Tonya's pregnant." Same way you'd say *Please pass the asparagus*.

It has, I'm sure, the desired effect. I blink. Darleen sucks in a breath.

"Got herself in a family way," Robert says, holding his eyes on mine. "Preggers."

He widens his eyes. "What else, Dad? A fertile Myrtle. A bun in the oven."

Robert takes a breath. "So the taxi driver lays on the horn, yells to the lady with the belly, 'Hey lady, you can get knocked *down*, too!'"

I keep blinking, and if Darleen hadn't slapped her hands against the table Robert might have kept going, all sayings I'd never once said to him. Except maybe the last. I vaguely remember that joke, sharing it with him despite the crudeness. Showing him I didn't think he was just a kid anymore.

After the jolting crack of Darleen's hands against the wood, we all sit and stare at each other. I know I have to say something, but all the wrong things crowd to get out: *Oh, so that's what's been keeping you busy; well, no wonder you've been preoccupied—baby showers, picking out names, finding a house.*

It's Darleen who finally asks, "Are you sure, Robert? How long have you known?"

Robert shrugs, his boldness deserting him. "A while."

"What are you going to do?" I say. No advice, no counseling, just dumping it on the shoulders of a sixteen-year-old. I look into my lap.

"I guess I'm going to marry her."

I keep looking at my lap, unable to bear it if he's glaring at me, turning his marriage, of all things, into a challenge to throw in my face.

Darleen whispers, "I thought maybe there were problems between you two."

Robert shrugs again, his universal answer. "Nope. No problems."

"But, Robert, getting married? You're only sixteen."

Robert rolls his eyes.

Trying to imagine what a father should say, I start, "But, Robert, just because you lost control, because you weren't careful." I'm stammering. "This shouldn't have to ruin the rest of your life. You have to face your responsibilities, but—"

Robert flushes. "I'm doing what's best for Tonya," he mutters. "I'm not ruining my life."

"But one mistake doesn't mean you have to rush into another," Darleen says. "There are options. If you two were on the outs, having a baby isn't going to make things better."

"We weren't 'on the outs' and I didn't make any mistakes!" Robert shouts. "All right? And I don't think marrying Tonya is another one!"

"Getting her pregnant wasn't a mistake?" I ask.

Robert glares at me. "I didn't get her pregnant! Okay?"

Again Darleen and I can only stare.

"How do you know?" I ask.

"Maybe I should give you The Talk, huh Dad? I mean, I know."

"Is that what Tonya says?" Darleen asks.

"I mean, I know!" Robert shouts.

"How can you be sure?" I ask.

"I know!" he shouts, standing so quickly his chair tips over, clattering on the tile he helped me put in only a few years ago.

He's near tears and he turns away so we won't see. Then he runs out the door. We hear his car rev up, skitter across the gravel of the drive, squeal in the street.

In the silence after the roar of his car, Darleen says, "Maybe they never had sex."

With all he shouted, it could be true, but as tight as they've been, I doubt it. What else could have held them so close, could have obliterated us so completely? "What was that all about then? Marrying her?"

Darleen shakes her head. "Being noble? Winning her back? I don't know."

"Do you think he knows who the father is?"

"Does it matter?"

"Do you think she knows?"

Darleen doesn't bother answering.

"I can't imagine anyone else squeezing between the two of them, let alone—"

"Maybe he really is the father," Darleen says quick enough to interrupt. "Maybe he just can't tell us."

I stand up, start to clear plates only half-emptied.

"I wonder if she knows about this," Darleen says. "His plans for them."

"You think he might have just said that?"

Darleen shrugs, rubbing at her forehead. "Maybe," she says. "The way you went after him."

"It's just," I start, but don't know what else to say. "This is what we were afraid of all along, isn't it? Since they started together. It's all come true."

Darleen stares at me. "I think the first thing you said, when he had a second date, was, 'Well, at least he's not gay.' "

"It was a joke," I answer.

"Like, 'Hey, lady, you can get knocked *down* too?' "

In bed that night, I lie straight as a board, listening for Robert's return. When he first learned to talk, I would come home from work every day and shout, "Who's my buddy, who's my pal?" and Robert would leap to the door, dancing with excitement.

"Bobbut!" he'd answer, thumping his fist against his chest, and I'd swing him into the air, saying, "You're not just whistling Dixie, Trixie."

Now I wonder about accidents, Robert driving in a fury, tears in his eyes, so disappointed with me he can't think, can't see. Everything out there he can't see.

Then I hear him, the return he'd devised when he'd been going out with Tonya long enough to make getting home on time impossible. The quiet rustle of his car, engine shut down two houses away, the gentle crunch of the gravel as he dead-sticks into the driveway, the click of the door, closed just enough to cut out the dome light, sparing the battery.

He glides up the steps, straight into his room.

"Darleen," I whisper. I don't know if she's sleeping or making me do this myself. I slip out of bed carefully, showing I don't want to wake her.

His door is closed, but light leaks underneath. I turn the knob carefully, and as I push the door open I have a tremor, wondering what I'll do if he has Tonya up here in his room, playing man and wife.

But Robert is sitting alone on the edge of his bed, elbows on knees, hands hanging limp before him. His bed is made. He hasn't even taken off his shoes. He doesn't turn my way.

"Did you see her?" I ask.

He twines his fingers together, bending them backward until a few knuckles pop. He says, "She doesn't want to marry me."

"She's a fool," I answer.

His face tightens.

"I mean she can't be thinking straight now. It's not you."

"That's a fact," he says. "She was pregnant way before she told me. She just didn't know whose it was."

"Does she now? Is it yours?"

"She says it's not just either-or." He quakes visibly. "She says there's a lot of possibilities."

"Do you think that's true?"

He finally turns his head far enough to look at me. "Do you think she'd just say that for fun?"

What I think is that maybe she's looked farther down this

grim road than Robert's let himself. But what I say is, "It's probably for the best. Getting wrapped up in something like that—"

"What are you talking about?" he spits. "Like this is good?"

I shake my head. "Not at all," I say. "I'm just glad you, that we'll be able . . ." I go quiet, take a big breath. "It's just that I—"

"You?" His eyes go wide. "You? This couldn't have less to do with you!" he blurts. "This is *my* life, Dad! My shitty, fucking, stinking life!"

I take a step back, involuntarily. He's looking at his shoes again, his hair dangling before his eyes.

"Okay," I say, edging out of his doorway. "Okay. I'm just glad you're home safe."

"Yeah," he mutters. "Home."

In the hallway our door stands blank and dark, open, and I picture Darleen poised on the edge of our bed, waiting. I turn away, creeping down the stairs, walking through our darkened house, every turn I know by heart.

In the driveway the old, beaten-down gravel is knobbledy beneath my bare feet, the breeze cool through my loose pajamas.

Robert's engine still ticks, the heat slowly fading. I touch the fender and walk back to his door. I lean against it, driving my hip into it until I hear the solid click of the latch. A trick from my own dating days, home too late, something I could have shown him.

Looking both ways down the quiet street where he has always lived, I say, "Bobbut!" and thump my fist against my chest, hard enough I feel my heart. "Bobbut!"

Wind

I'm blowing smoke out the cracked bathroom window, Susie
Fields and Debbie Monahan at the sinks behind me, giggling
over makeup, vigilantly ignoring me. Outside the wind shifts,
catching the parking-lot stop sign so it starts to shimmy, shaking like it's having some kind of fit. A shudder ripples through
me, too, and I stub my cigarette quick against the glass. Sometimes, I figure, I must look as jittery as that sign, the idea of
blowing out of here whipping through me. It's all I ever think
about.

So this year, when the new guy shows up, like a gift, I
know what I have to do. On one hand I can count the new
people who've moved here, and them just drifting from ranch
to ranch. But Kirk's way different than any of them.

Can you imagine moving from Seattle to here? The dis-
appointment?

Poor guy's dad made a scad of money somehow, so with
the whole world to choose from, they moved here. To the

mountains, they thought, but overshooting by about fifty miles. Landing out here in the plains, it might as well have been fifty thousand.

Kirk's pretty weird—the whole grunge thing; baggy clothes, little wispy beard under the middle of his lip—but I'm on him like stink. It's not like I can't see a ticket out when it falls in my lap. First time I talk to him he's in the cafeteria, sitting as alone as you can get under the huge red bucking bronc mural. *Go Red Riders!* God.

He's surprised anybody's talking to him, then looks plenty happy to see it's me. I mean, I'm no scarecrow.

First thing he asks, making conversation, is, "Is it always this windy here?"

I bust out laughing. I mean, it's practically calm anyway—probably not blowing more than twenty, twenty-five. But I say, "That's the only thing we got going for us. We'll blow away soon enough."

He looks at me.

"Not soon enough," I admit. "No such thing as that."

"You don't like it here?" he asks.

My eyes about roll out of my head. "Do you?"

He smiles a little. "Yeah," he says. "It sucks all right."

That same night I drag him down to the motel me and Mom run and we do it in the little shed out back, Dad's old wood shop. It's hunting season, so there isn't a vacant room. It's not the most comfortable spot, but I've survived it before, and I'm not giving anybody else a chance at Kirk.

While the wind rattles the windows, sneaking in through every crack, touching me places I shouldn't ever shiver, Kirk pokes away like he's never done it before. I try to help, but mainly I'm just wishing he'd hurry. I scrunch up my nose against the stench of old mouse turds and sawdust and sex. I think how there hasn't been a tool lifted in here since I was fourteen, since the day Dad left, and I wonder again how he stuck it out as long as he did. I moan a couple times for Kirk's sake, still wishing Dad had at least asked if I wanted to come along.

Finally Kirk straightens out and gives his little shiver, just like a brained trout, and then slumps across me. I stare out at the empty gloom, the place barely lit by the yard light, the windows crusted thick with dust. Eventually I push him off, scrunching at whatever's been digging into my shoulder, some old scrap of Dad's.

After that night, Kirk's as steady around me as the wind. Turns out that *was* his first time. Can you believe that? I mean, God, no wonder! Him with his Nirvana clothes and all. I could've laid there like a plank.

So now he's like a kid with the cookie jar, and sometimes I let him, and sometimes I keep the lid on. Drives him right to the edge. I mean, if I told Kirk to walk through a mile of fire, on his belly, on broken glass, I mean he'd do it that fast. For me.

Driving around in the brand-new, three-quarter-ton Ford his dad bought for him, he keeps telling me I'm the most beautiful thing he's ever seen, the most special, but I don't let him talk like that much. Not unless I'm down or something, when that kind of stuff isn't so bad to hear, no matter how ridiculous. Instead I make him tell me about Seattle, and San Francisco, where it turns out he lived before Seattle. Only makes it worse, you know? San Francisco, then Seattle, then here. God!

He starts hearing a little about me, around school maybe, or maybe I let down my guard, drop a few things myself. Anyway, he develops this jealous streak about ten miles wide, thinking about me before he got here. As we drive out of town one night, he asks, "Who did you used to go out with?"

Go out with? I think. Who says that? I tell him to take a left onto the stringy little dirt road cutting up the side of the bluff. I say, "That's not what you need to worry about."

"What do you mean?" he asks, worried and mad at the same time. Like a trained dog. Jumping through hoops.

"I mean, there wasn't anything you could do about that. We didn't even know each other then."

I tell him where to park, a few small lights way out below. He keeps pestering, so I give him a kiss and start working at his belt buckle. He doesn't know we're at the old buffalo jump Dad found, where the Indians chased the buffalo off the cliffs before they had horses. Only Dad and I know about this place. As I straddle him, see his face go stupid, I think of the bones surrounding us, yards deep. All those buffalo charging right off the cliffs.

Afterward, heading home, he keeps nagging: who, when, where. So, finally I tell him about Mom finding my diary. "It wasn't a very smart thing for me to keep lying around," I say, though I guess I didn't really mind Mom finding it.

"What was in it?" he asks, poking his tongue around his lips, like he's gone dry as all those old bones.

"Pretty much everything," I say. "Didn't leave much out."

"Like what?" he whispers, driving along in the dark.

"I don't know how much she read, but it was all there."

"What?"

"Hello?" I say. "Earth to Kirk. I mean, do you want me to spell it out for you?" I give him a squeeze. "I mean, by now I'd think you'd have a pretty good idea."

I'm pushing him maybe too hard. He's gripping the steering wheel like it might get away from him, take him someplace he doesn't want to go.

"It started with the first, and just kept going," I say, petting his leg.

"Who was first?" It sounds like he's strangling.

"Nobody you know."

"Who?"

"Just some guy at the motel. I cleaned his room."

"When?" He manages to breathe.

"What do you mean, when? At night. After Mom was asleep."

Kirk drives a while. Finally he says, "How old were you?"

"Oh, hell. I don't know. It was a long time ago."

"We're only seventeen."

"For crying out loud, Kirk, what difference does it make?" I take my hand away from him. "I don't know. Fourteen maybe."

It was the night after the day Dad left. I know exactly.

"When you were fourteen?" He sounds like he's been kicked. "How old was he?"

"I didn't ask," I say. "Older." I try to laugh. "I mean, he was driving already. He was staying in motels." We've done it in a few of the motel rooms, and I think that might cheer him up, thinking about that. But it doesn't work that way.

"Did he know how old you were?" he says. "Did he know he was your first?"

"He might've thought I was older," I whisper, trying to think of some way to change the subject.

"Did he know he was your first?" he asks again.

"Hell!" I shout. "How should I know? It wasn't some big romance." I remember using my pass key, walking straight into his room. How startled he was.

"I was just sick of everybody talking about it," I say. " 'When are you going to do it?' 'How long should you save it?' 'Till some perfect prom?' 'For your husband?'—some guy they're all sure they're going to spend the rest of their pathetic lives with. All of them with about as much of a chance as those buffalo flying off the cliffs."

I stare at the dash. He doesn't know what I'm talking about. "I just got tired of it," I say.

Kirk swallows, keeps driving.

I think of that guy in the motel, asking me what I thought I was doing. Asking me to leave. Me undoing my shirt, my fingers shaking so bad I could barely open the buttons. Knowing Dad wasn't ever coming back. I remember him watching, and then, at last, his shrug. I haven't thought of this in a long, long time.

"Just forget it, all right?" I say to Kirk.

I fold my arms tight across my front, but I can't stand it. "Shit!" I shout, smashing my hands against the dash. "I thought we might just be able to talk! I thought you might be old enough to handle a little adult conversation!"

Pretty soon he's apologizing, saying again that the idea of me with anyone else just makes him crazy. How I'm so special he can't bear the thought of somebody just using me for sex.

Using me? I think, and shake my head.

I keep listening for a while—even after he parks out front of the motel, the truck getting cold. Then I say, "What we need to do is get out of this place, Kirk. It's making you as crazy as the rest of them."

"What?" he says.

"It's the wind. It drives people nuts."

"Only thing I'm nuts about is you," he says. He smiles. We're making up.

Finally I say, "I gotta run. Maybe Mom even noticed I'm gone."

Kirk stops me for a kiss, but after I give him a quick one, he still holds on. I've explained to him how I can't stand that, can't stand anybody holding me that way, stopping me. I knock his hand away.

He blurts, "Sorry," but then says, "What'd she do?"

"Who?"

"Your mom?"

"What?"

He swallows, turns a second to look out the window. His face glimmers red in the neon of our motel sign. "The diary."

"Oh." I whistle. "That wasn't pretty. But once she shouted herself out, she marched me into Great Falls, to the clinic. The pill. Stacks of safe-sex pamphlets. She hasn't talked about it since."

I can hear Kirk's teeth grinding. "Was your dad still alive then?" he whispers.

I shake my head quick. He only asked about him once before, and it's not something I ever talk about. I mean, I told him he was dead and all. "Mom blamed him for it, of course," I say. "I mean, like it was him I was fucking or something."

Kirk jerks like I zapped him with a cattle prod. "He was dead, Wendy," he whispers.

I nod. "I got to go," I say. When I swing open the door, we both blink, stopped by the glare of the cab light. Turning toward the dimmer light of the motel—the sickly glow that's cut across my bedroom my whole life, *Mountain View Motel*—I say, "See you tomorrow," and run for the door.

But I don't see Kirk tomorrow, or just barely, dodging around the halls in school. I sit through class; watch Mr. Ivanosec dig out earwax with the end of his pen; listen to the wind blast the dirt and sand against the brick and windows, scouring away.

I don't see Kirk more than that, those hallway dodges, for the rest of the week.

He's avoiding me, I realize.

Bullshit on that, I say to myself. Bullshit on that.

When Kirk's dad answers my knock, I catch his look. It's quick, he's good, but I figure I've seen it often enough at the motel. The *Whooee!* look.

I've got to admit, I'm dressed to stun—my top low enough to leave nothing to doubt, my skirt high enough to do the same, and tight enough you can read the brand of my panties. At least that's what Mom yelled after me as I left the motel—a rare outburst of parenting. It's colder than hell out, but I'd opened my parka on the porch, so Kirk would get an eyeful of what he's been missing right off.

"Is Kirk around?" I ask when his dad doesn't do anything but stand there.

"Sure," he says. "Sure." He stands back to let me in. I can feel him watching my ass. I am sure glad he is not my father.

But the smoky warmth inside is like this huge hello, and right away I see the woodstove, the splintery white logs beside it, like I've walked into a Christmas card, these guys doing their living-in-the-mountains thing. Nothing like the burned-dust smell of the electric baseboards at the motel.

"You must be Wendy," Kirk's dad says.

"And you must be Kirk's dad."

"Dwight," he says, holding out his hand.

Then Kirk's there, before I have a chance to take his dad's

hand. He looks pouty in his huge jeans and untucked flannel shirt. "Hey," he says.

I shake his dad's hand. Kirk just stands there.

"Don't tell me you forgot?" I say.

That smacks him. We don't have a thing planned. How could we, when he ducks into a classroom every time he sees me?

"Forgot what?" he says.

"About our date? The movie?" I roll my eyes. "Hello? Steven Seagal?"

Kirk shuffles there, a deer in the headlights.

I look at his dad. "Is he always this spacey?"

He shrugs and smiles. "I haven't seen that much of him since he met you."

I smile back, like it's a compliment.

Kirk says he's going to get another shirt and slips out of the room. I take a step away from his dad and try to remember what Kirk told me about his mom. I know she's not around, but I can't remember why.

"So," I say, just so I'm not standing there like another chunk of firewood. "How do you like it here so far?"

"It's been a good move for us," he says.

I look around the room, searching for some trace; doilies or knickknacks, the kind of stuff Mom used to clutter around our place when she was trying to make a home. But there's nothing like that. Just some books, a coat thrown over the back of a chair, a blanket on the couch that looks like it gets used.

"Have you spent your entire life here?" the dad asks.

I spin back like he caught me spying. Spent? I think. Not a dime. I'm saving for my future. "Hasn't everybody?" I ask. "I mean, except you?"

He tilts his head, smiles again.

I look at him, then away. I hate the way old men smile. I'm beginning to wonder if Kirk crawled out a window somewhere, ran off into the snow. But he shuffles in then, like somebody's pushing him. "You ready then?"

"Have been," I say. But, though he's hardly in a hurry, he gets to the door before I do.

"Nice meeting you," I say to Kirk's dad. Kirk jiggles the doorknob.

"The way Kirk talks, I'm sure we'll be seeing a lot of you," he answers.

I bet you'd like that, I think, but I give him a little wave and say, "Bye."

"Be careful!" he yells as Kirk swooshes the door shut behind us.

On the porch, without taking a step, Kirk says, "I never said anything about any movie."

"Who cares?" I say. "We had to say something. Let's get in the truck at least. It's freezing out here."

I hear him crunching across the snow after me and I hop into the cab. The seat's hard and searing cold on the back of my thighs, even with the nylons.

I rub my hands up and down my legs as he revs the engine.

He turns and looks at me and I say, "You could do this for me if you want."

"I'm all right," he murmurs, and backs away from the house.

The movie theater in town, no matter what the OPENING SOON sign says, has been closed since I was ten, and Kirk drives straight out toward Great Falls, even after I tell him there's plenty of vacancies at the motel. Before I know it, we're driving past Freezeout, the lake where all the geese stop on their way through. Sometimes it's white with them. Now it's frozen solid, the top dull and silvery in the moonlight. The reeds and stuff poke up black around the edges. There's not a living thing left out there.

Kirk hasn't said a word, and I'm not sure how to handle this little uprising. Finally I decide to go for it all. I say, "Let's keep going."

He glances away from the flat shimmer of the road. "What?"

"Let's not go back. Let's go to Seattle. Or San Francisco."

He stares at me so long I touch the wheel, keeping us on the road. "You got to be careful here," I warn. "There's deer all over."

"Just leave?" he asks. "That's your plan?"

"Like there's something here to keep us?"

"What would we do then? Once we weren't here?"

"Anything. Whatever. I mean, it's not like your dad'll let us starve."

"Really?" he says, taking his foot off the gas. Pretty soon he pulls off the road at the buildings for the guys who work at the lake. Nobody'll be here till spring though, when the birds come back. Even with our windows up tight, the engine running, you can hear some metal banging, a piece of siding torn half-off by the wind.

He shuts down the lights and the lake is in front of us, spooky-looking it's so flat and blank, like it's sponging up all the moonlight. The wind rocks the truck on its springs. Riffles of ground snow tear across the ice. Next stop, the Dakotas. There is like no end to the nothing out here.

"So that's your plan," he mumbles at the windshield. "Just use that money to get out of here."

I scooch over next to him. "Not just me," I whisper. "Both of us. You and me. Together."

He barely puts his arm around me, so I go for his pants, figuring I can still make him take me wherever I want to go.

He puts his hand over mine though, twisting away a little, pulling the button out of my fingers.

"What?" I say. I've already slid halfway to the floor. It is not a comfortable position for a conversation. "What is your problem lately?" I go back to work on his fly.

"Don't," he says.

I throw myself back onto the seat, against my door. "Great," I say. "Like what? You've been called to the priest-hood?"

He doesn't say anything. Just stares out at the lake. About the coldest-looking thing in the universe right now. The metal bangs behind us and I think of that stop sign. I am this close to getting out of here.

"What?" I say again, louder this time.

He runs his fingers back and forth on the steering wheel. "We wouldn't have a dime if it wasn't for Mom," he mumbles. "Lately I've been wondering what she'd think of me now. About all of this."

"What do you mean?" I ask. "Where is she anyway?"

That stumps him. He turns to me. "My mom? What?"

"I don't remember," I tell him.

He stares a second before murmuring, "She's dead. That's why we left Seattle. It was too hard being where . . ." He stops, glancing at the lake. "You couldn't remember that?"

I give a whistle. "Died? Mean, like really dead?"

He puts both his hands on the wheel. "What other way is there?" he asks, sounding as empty as the lake.

"Well, there's dead like my dad. Alive somewhere, but same as dead to me."

He looks at me. "You told me—"

"As good as," I say. "That's what I meant. He might as well be, I mean. You know?"

"No," he says. "There is no such thing as being like dead. You don't know a thing."

"Sorry," I say, and when he just keeps staring at me, I say, "Okay? I'm sorry. Sorry I even brought it up."

"You don't even know all you don't know," he says.

I think I once said that very same thing to him. When we were first doing it. Teasing him, leading him on.

"I know we have to get out of here," I say, still hoping.

"All those guys you let fuck you," he says, still choking on the word, "were those all the same? Hoping they'd take you away? From the first one? When you were fourteen. Were you just hoping he'd take you with him?"

"Listen, Kirk!" I say, jabbing a finger at him. "Nobody has ever fucked me!"

He looks down at my finger, then out the side window, completely away from me.

"And I don't need anybody to take me out of here!" I shout. "I can go anytime I want! It's not like there's anything stopping me. Anything holding me back."

"Then why don't you go?" He looks at me again, in what gray light leaks through the window. "What are you so afraid of? Or do you need Mom's settlement money?"

He looks outside. "You can have that," he says.

I wonder about that a second, then he says, "Why didn't you just go with your dad, if you hated it here so bad? Why didn't he take you with him?"

"Fuck you!" I shout. I'm punching him before he knows it. Before I know it. "Fuck you!" I keep screaming. Like some kind of crazy person.

He pushes me away finally, gentle as he can, really. I mean, considering. I fling open my door, fling a last, "Fuck you, Captain Kirk!" at him, and throw myself out of the truck.

But my jacket's inside, and out here it's like stepping into a blast furnace made for cold, not heat. With what I'm wearing it's the same as being naked, freezing needles driving into me everywhere, blowing straight through me, turning me to ice. I can't live out here, I think. I can't survive it.

When I whip open Kirk's door, it's the last thing he expects. He's leaning over toward my door, maybe still trying to stop me, maybe locking me out, who knows? But I catch him off guard, grab him by the collar and fling him to the frozen ground before he can gasp, "Wendy?"

I step on him, which is risky. He grabs my ankle, but I get a grip like iron on the steering wheel. Already, just running around his truck, I feel like I've got about two seconds left to live if I don't get back into the heat.

My free foot connects with all I got. He knows better than to grab me like that. I feel a crunch, and Kirk gurgles out this funny little cry. I couldn't say whether I hit him in the face or crotch. But he isn't holding me back anymore, and I'm in the truck, chattering backward over the frosted grass, turning away so I don't run over him.

I hit the lights in time to see him start to stand up, so I'm guessing it wasn't crotch. I've had to do that before in the motel, and believe me, they don't just pop back up.

Then I'm whipping past the buildings, the truck wound out loud enough I finally can't hear that banging metal. The cattle guard rocks me and then I'm on pavement, heading out at full speed, in a brand-new, paid-for, three-quarter-ton Ford.

Kirk will be all right, I think. It's not like they made those buildings like some high-security prison. He'll break in before he freezes. There'll be a phone in there. And then he's got that home to go back to, his dad, that fire. He'll be fine.

Me, I'm out of here. At last.

But even though I'm finally on my way, the road is bleary

before me, the start of tears making everything swim. I try to think of how, if I stayed here, the frozen wind would turn the tears to ice, blind me forever, but all I can think of is that stupid fire back in Kirk's house, big dumb Dwight sitting there waiting for him, waiting to hear how his date went, waiting so they can both fill in that hole his mom left.

I swipe at my tears and look hard for deer, which can be practically as black as the night. I wish I knew where my dad was.

But all I really know is that Kirk is still just standing there in the cold, just standing there alone watching me leave, not quite believing this is happening to him. I know exactly how that goes.

My foot falters toward the brake. Then, instead, I shove down the gas, wondering why Dad couldn't have taken the time to think of me standing that way.

"Goddamn it!" I shout, hitting the dash, stomping the brakes at the same time. I wonder what Kirk, standing there in the freezing, whistling wind, will think when he sees the white back-up lights flash on.

The engine howls as I gun it in reverse, weaving back down the road, bouncing over the cattle guard. I can hardly see anything and I hope he's got the sense to get out of the way. The truck slides to a stop on the frozen ground, the dead, matted grass, the traces of snow.

I leave it running, the noise blocking out at least a part of the wind's victory howls. I can barely breathe and I hear the click of the passenger-door latch, Kirk whispering my name—"Wendy?"—like it's the biggest question in the world.

Almost as big as me asking if I can stay in their house tonight. At least this one night. Please.

The Thatch Weave

Dad steps into my room, but stops just inside the door, the smell of model glue and paint smacking him cold. "That was your mother," he says, his voice hoarse. "The baby's had another bad night."

I knew it was Mom as soon as the phone rang. She calls the same time every morning. From the hospital down in Salt Lake. I paint the last trailing wisp of camouflage across the rudder.

"Adam," Dad says. Quiet. "Did you hear me?"

I nod once, put my brush in the thinner jar. The sky blue underside is already dry and I hold it there, arc the heavy fighter through a wing-over, pushing the stall limits.

"This isn't something you can just ignore, Adam. You're almost ten years old and—"

I straighten out the fighter, a daring head-on attack. Who blinks first? "A P-47 Thunderbolt," I say. "The Flying Jug."

"Don't start," Dad says.

"Able to withstand more battle damage than any fighter ever built," I answer.

"Adam!"

"Out-dive anything in the skies. Except maybe an anvil. For ground attack there—"

Faster than I can jerk back my plane, Dad's at my desk. I can see how hard he's shaking just glancing at his shirt cuffs.

"She is not a plane!" he yells. "She's your sister!"

"Wingman," I correct. "Shadowing my every move. Watching my tail."

Dad's fist slams down right on top of my Chance Vought Corsair, the gullwing master of the Pacific skies. It's a direct hit, no hope for a parachute.

Pulling my Thunderbolt close to my chest, I stare at the broken plane. Dad's never broken anything of mine in his life. "Total failure to employ the Thatch weave," I whisper.

"What?" Dad bellows.

"The Thatch weave." It's the tactic Jimmy Thatch invented—two Wildcats always turning into the faster, nimbler Japanese Zeros, covering each other, surviving until the Hellcat came along, making them the faster, nimbler ones. I use my hands, showing how it works. "As long as we employ the Thatch weave, nothing can touch us."

He shouts something and his other fist comes down, blowing my dreaded Focke Wulf FW 190 to smithereens. I dodge my Thunderbolt into cloud cover behind my back.

In one huge sweep, Dad sends everything flying off my desk—glue, paint, X-Acto knives, broken planes. "She's your sister!" he shouts again. He stands there a second, doing damage assessment, then spins and heads back to his base.

I know who Jessica is, though I only saw her once, the day she was born. Mom's been with her in Salt Lake ever since.

She's not even two weeks old, though that's older than they said she'd get.

I turn my desk around, facing away from the door, but I feel when Dad steps inside again. I hear when he rubs his face, the scraping of his black whisker stubble. After a while he says, "So, I says to myself, I says . . ."

I don't turn around. I'm painting white and black stripes on the wings of my Thunderbolt. Invasion stripes. So in the heat of battle over Normandy the good guys will see who their friends are. Not take anybody out with friendly fire.

He keeps waiting. I know he won't go away until I answer, so finally I say, "So I says to myself, I says, '*Self.*' "

"That's right!" he says, as if I hadn't waited even a second. "I says to myself, I says, 'Self, you have got a pile of work to do.' "

"So you better get after it," I answer.

"Darn tooting!" Dad cries.

I flip the Thunderbolt over, painting the bottom of the wings. Dad watches me.

He lets out a long, loud breath. "So," he says.

"So you better get after it," I say again.

The models he smashed, the FW 190 and the Corsair, two of the most feared fighters of the war, lie in the trash can right beside my desk.

After a little while more, he leaves. Pretty soon I hear the mower crank up, hear him start the revolutions of the yard.

The yard is my job, but I pull the shade down and finish the invasion stripes. Standing on my bed, I set the P-47 on the top shelf to dry, then prop up a book in front of it. But Dad could probably find it anyway. He's probably got radar. Like a night fighter. A Heinkel 219 Owl.

. . .

Dad's sweating by the time he sees me watching him. He's stranded in the center of the yard, the mowed grass surrounding him, nothing left uncut. He flips the switch and that fast you can hear the street again; another mower going a block over, some car someplace, kids yelling a long way off.

"This exercise is supposed to be good for you," he says, wiping at his forehead, making a play stagger to the side.

Five and a half miles above us, the B-17 Flying Fortresses open their yawning bomb bays. The bombardiers look through their Norden bombsights, the crosshairs steady on the top of Dad's sweat-slicked black hair. Then the bombs begin their wobbling, whistling flight, whole sticks of them laddering down the sky. Our street goes up like the Schweinfurt ball-bearing works, the Ploesti oil refineries. The explosions begin at the corner and walk up the block, throwing the elms, the cars, the mowers—Dad, me, everything—sky-high.

I stare at him. At where his hands wrap around the worn-out rubber on the mower handle. He starts over toward me. The mower bounces over the ground, though it looks smooth and soft.

He goes right past me, smelling like hot, wet, broken grass and gasoline. The mower rattles onto the driveway. I look up and down the street, the sun sifting through the green tunnels of the elms.

As he starts the backyard, I sit down on the edge of the lawn, waiting for the first bomb at the corner.

In a while I hear the mower quit, then listen to Dad's steps close in on me. I draw my head closer to my shoulders, hunkering down in the bomb shelter. He stops next to me. I can see his shoes, the grass blades sticking to them. The B-17s, clawing through the fighter cover, are late.

"I'm sorry," he says, just standing there.

He doesn't even move his feet.

"I'm sorry about this morning," he says.

I see Dad's cuffs jerk up, know he's getting ready to sit down. Then he's there in the damp grass right next to me.

"Doesn't help, does it?" he asks.

I look down the street. The B-17s, unescorted this deep into enemy territory, are getting chewed up by the fighters; FW 190s, Me 109s, maybe even 110s with their cannons. The gunners swivel every which way, tracers cutting the sky, trying to follow the streaking, flashing dives of the tiny fighters. The bombs, if any of them make it through, could land anywhere.

"It's just . . ." Dad says. He's rubbing his stubble again.

"Maybe you should shave," I say. A bomb lands blocks and blocks away. Not even collateral damage.

He quits rubbing his face. "It's just," he says, "this isn't going to work the way you're doing it." He stops again. Then goes. "We've got to pull together, Adam. Till Mom gets back."

He doesn't say till Mom *and Jessica* get back.

"You can't keep hiding this way," Dad says. "You can't pretend we're all planes, that this is some sort of combat, something we can fight through, can win."

He waits, then says, "You've got to help me fill in for Mom while she's gone," Dad says.

The bomber crews went through this same sort of resentment, the soldiers only seeing their coddling on the ground, not knowing the terror of daylight bombing, of being nothing more than a flying target. "I don't know how to cook," I say.

Dad stares at me a second. "I never said anything about cooking."

"I don't know how to do laundry," I say.

"I'm not asking you to do laundry. I'm not asking you to

cook. I just don't want you hunched over your models every day, like nothing is going on at all. You can't just pretend this isn't happening, Adam."

He's getting worked up again. I'm glad I hid the Thunderbolt.

"I just don't need any more of your planes," Dad says. "The Thatch weave or whatever."

The Thatch weave saved hundreds of lives. I don't bother explaining it again.

I hear Dad take a big breath, blow it out. "Do you want to call Mom?" he asks.

I pick some of the fragments of mown grass off my hands. A Flying Fortress, so high above us, takes a direct hit in the bomb bay, the whole plane vanishing in a flash that blinds the crews of the bombers around it.

He takes one more of those breaths. "Adam," he says. "I'm sorry about your models. I never should have done that. I just, I was, it . . ." He looks down the street. "I'll buy you new models. Will that make it better?"

Will that bring the pilots back? I think.

Dad stands up, giving my shoulder a tap. "Come on, buddy," he says. "Let's run out to Hobby Land."

The all-clear whistle sounds. Only that one bomb, a clean miss. A lot of empty beds at the airfield in England tonight.

We're almost to the car when we hear the phone ring. It's Mom, and he winds up talking till dinnertime, the post-mission debriefing. We never make it to Hobby Land.

The next morning, when I wake up, the new models are on my bed. He must've gone out in the middle of the night. I look at the boxes, still tight in plastic wrap. A Brewster Buffalo and a P-39 Bell Airacobra. Two of the most miserable fighters ever produced. Our pilots were sitting ducks in them. I can't even believe he found kits. Who'd ever buy them? And to replace an FW 190? A Corsair?

I sit in my pajamas, staring at the two boxes. Once, this pilot over New Guinea bailed out of his P-39 just because he *saw* a Zero. That's how much good they were. Had a better chance down in the jungle, alone with the snakes and the headhunters.

Dad's downstairs at the table when I come down. He's on the phone again, and he's crying. He still hasn't shaved.

I go to the refrigerator and open the door, pretending I'm looking for juice. It's right there on the table next to him. I hide behind the door so I can't see him. I listen to the roar of the B-17 engines, the big Wright Cyclones warming up for another try today. They drown out everything.

But then Dad's there next to me, nudging me out of the way so he can close the refrigerator. The cold air is falling around me. At thirty thousand feet it's thirty below. Casualties freeze in their own blood.

"She's gone," he says. "Jessica's gone."

He waits. "Mom will be home tomorrow," he tells me.

He pats my head, tries to flatten out my hair.

I see the tracers arcing in, chewing into the cowling, walking back toward the cockpit, my stick jammed, ailerons shot away. "Even through the Thatch weave," I whisper.

Dad shouts, his voice cracking, "Your sister is dead! Do you even hear what I'm saying? Do you?"

Side-slipping, I'm out the front door before he can catch me. I fly down the street, so low I'm beneath the canopy of the elms, leaves and branches snapping off against my leading edge. My Thunderbolt is hit hard, smoking, oil streaking back from the holes in the cowling. But she'll get me home. It's what they built the P-47 to do.

My sister's pathetic Bell Airacobra gives only one quick flash in the dense green of the jungle. I take my Thunderbolt as high as I dare, the wings shuddering with the strain. There's not a chute anywhere, the sky empty and pale.

Burning precious gasoline, I circle once, making sure. Then I waggle my wings in salute, set my nose down, lean out the mixture, and begin the long, slow descent, bringing my crippled bird back alone.

The Gravy on the Cake

The leaving was only ever for work. Dad made sure we knew that. "Just pounding the pavement, Mame," he'd say, though he never worked a day in a city in his life. "Just putting the bacon in the bank." With one last kiss he'd be off. "You girls cover your backs."

Before his truck disappeared down the street, Mom would be diving headlong into something new. Some hobby or something to fill the hole. The way they glued on to each other when he was home, it must've been a gaper. A regular Grand Canyon.

Once she decided to take up knitting. Probably figured she'd make some warm stuff for him out in the woods. Socks, scarves, who knows, maybe she pictured whole sweaters— chest, back, arms, cuffs, collars, the entire shooting match.

But Mom had to go whole hog, of course. I come home from high school, this was only a couple years ago, freshman year, and there's this black-faced, dirty-wooled sheep eating our lawn. I stand outside the listing, paint-peeling pickets of our fence and stare at it.

"Baa," I say.

It munches away, hardly giving me a glance.

Now, Great Falls is not like the world or anything, but it's still not someplace you keep a sheep. I glance up and down the block, open the gate, and slip through. I am so glad I learned to stop bringing anyone to this house.

I leave the gate open. Start herding the sheep toward it. But it lets me bump right into it, goes right on tugging at the grass. "Go on, sheep," I grunt, pushing at its greasy wool with both hands, all my weight. "Take a powder."

But, seeing the one thing Dad never could, this sheep knows what a deal it's got here. It's not going anywhere, even if it has to carry me around like a cowboy.

"Come on, sheep-for-brains," I say, giving it a little bit of a kick. "Make a break for it. Hit the road." Dad'd say something like, "Make a road for it. Hit the powder."

Then Mom appears on the porch. Or maybe she's been standing there all along. "We'll shear after dinner, Luce," she says.

She's holding the electric clippers Dad used on me when I was just a kid. Crewcuts. Like, if he could trim close enough, he might somehow be able to nip the leg off that second X chromosome of mine, shave it down to a Y. Boys-R-Us. Spent my entire childhood looking just like his pictures of himself as a kid. Like some death camp survivor.

As a little girl, I sat docile through the haircuts, waiting for Mom to step in, to say, "Come on, Chuck, she's a girl." Waiting for her to slide up to him as he clipped on the plastic wing that'd keep my hair an even overall quarter-inch long. The motorboat, he called it, calling the haircut *going waterskiing,* hamming it up with jumps over my ears, carving turns around the spine bump, roaring outboard noises the whole time. Sometimes even I couldn't keep in a giggle, though it was my head, my hair. But I never stopped waiting for Mom to slide her hands over his shoulders, down his chest, maybe inside his shirt. "Let's you and me go make that boy of yours," I pictured her whispering. Then, after they slipped off, my plan was to motorboat that old clipper right into the tree, full swing at the end of its cord. A terrible mishap. A waterskiing disaster. Not survivor one.

But, when he was clipping my hair he was home, there's no denying that, and Mom wasn't ever going to do anything to monkey-wrench that. I had to stand up for myself. Believe me, I wasn't going to go through puberty, my whole life, looking like Sinead O'Connor. Finally I wore a bike helmet when he came home, clamping it down tight whenever he caught me in his sights, asking what I wanted to do. Even when he was home we always had to be going somewhere, doing something. He laughed and laughed when I told him what the helmet was for, saying he had the safest kid in the world, a regular Fort Knox of a kid.

Yeah, I thought, a Fort Knox with curls.

He only stayed a couple days that time before loading his chainsaws back into his truck, the exhaust blowing all frosty and gray into the cold dawn, a smoke ring puffing out now and then. He patted me on the helmet, said, "Later, Tater."

"Adios, amoebas," I answered.

He hummed something for a minute, just standing there, and then, out of the blue, said, "You don't have to wear that helmet, Luce. You don't like the buzz, all you had to do was say."

I tightened the chin strap. "Just playing it safe," I said.

He was waiting, I knew, for Mom and the big good-bye. She dressed to kill for these few seconds, and though she was never late, I guessed she must be putting on a few drop-dead finishing touches. "Something for him to keep in mind," she told me once as I sat beside her on her bed, watching her strip out of the nylons she'd only worn for a few minutes.

I leaned against her arm. "He couldn't ever forget you," I answered, picturing them in the street, wrapped so tight a sheet of air wouldn't squeeze between. "Not the way you say good-bye."

She stood up, wriggling out of her slip, letting it crumple around her ankles. "It's what we do best," she agreed.

"Practice makes perfect."

She looked down at me on the bed. "You sound just like him." She shook her head. "Little as you see him, you sound just the same."

But today, standing waiting for her, Dad suddenly says, "Don't ever think it was you, Bug."

I glance up from under the neon bridge of my helmet. "What?"

"Just don't think that. When I'm gone, every time, I'm not just coming back for your mom."

This after Mom and him spend almost his whole visit locked in her room, like sunlight holds some rare peril for them. First time we didn't do one thing, go anywhere.

I start a little grin, waiting for the punch line. "Okay."

"I always did what I could," he says. "Don't forget that."

"Sure, Dad," I say. I mean, he's standing there patting the helmet I'm wearing to keep him from mowing me bald.

I glance up and down the dawn-dark street. "Where is Mom?" I ask at last.

"I don't expect her this morning," he says, like it's the most natural thing in the world.

"Of course we expect her," I say. "We just hope she's not expecting."

He grudges out a little smile.

" 'Less it's a boy, of course," I add.

He nods. "Of course," he answers, still without a trace of heart in it.

If he's not waiting for Mom, I don't know why he's hanging around for this. I never could whip out his sayings the way he could. Nobody on earth could quite do that.

Then out comes Mom. She's not dressed up though, not slinking out like some dish in an old-time movie. She just shuffles out in her robe, like anybody else on this street might, tired and grumbly, wanting nothing but the morning paper.

But she slides into his arms like usual, even opening her robe for his hands right there on the street, though it's so early there's no one up in the world except us.

"Guy's gotta work, Mame," I hear him whisper into her hair.

She nods, but answers, "Guy's gotta do a whole hell of a lot more than that."

"You guys gotta eat."

"Ditto," she answers.

Then they break apart, like they've already been down that road too often. Dad chucks me under the chin, says, "See you later, crocodile."

"After a while, alligator," I answer.

Then he's gone, Mom and me watching his truck disappear, then just standing there shivering. After a while, Mom says, "Take the helmet off, Luce. Christ, you look like a nutcase."

"A hairy one," I answer, unbuckling the strap.

The older I got, the less Dad came home, though I don't know if I had anything to do with that or not. Maybe just coincidence. Me growing up as they fell apart. After the helmet, it got to where we'd see him maybe once, twice a year.

But he never forgot us. He always sent money. A steady stream of hokey postcards. "The weather is here, wish you were beautiful." Then he'd write, "Just kidding," like we didn't know that, like we hadn't lived with him, on and off, our whole lives.

With Dad hardly ever there, his arrivals something we almost stopped expecting, an uncle or two started dropping by, spending the night. Mom said she just couldn't stand it anymore, being so alone. I don't know why she bothered with the *uncle* bit, though. Uncles of love, I called them.

Afterward, I'd police the place, wiping out any clues. I mean, you still had to hope Dad might drop back in. Once, spending all morning screwing up my nerve, I stood in front of Mom at the kitchen table, holding a cigarette butt in front of her face. "Least you could do is cover your tracks," I told her. "Nobody here smokes."

She looked up at me as if I was some total stranger. "I might have a smoke now and then," she said. "I might just take it up. You never know what I might do."

After Dad's last visit, the quickest on record, cut short in the middle of the night, Mom telling me in the morning that he'd had to leave early, what Mom swan-dives into is cooking. From a history of Rice-a-Roni and Shake-and-Bake, Taco John's and Wendy's, suddenly she's some kind of gourmet. Okay. But, truth is, she couldn't cook her way out of a paper bag. If Dad was here, he'd get laughing till he couldn't stop, squeaking out things like, "Cooking? Mame? That'd be the gravy on the cake." I know he'd say that. "Wouldn't that just take the icing?"

But it's been months since that last visit, and the only trace of Dad's been those postcards from the timber. Last one from British Columbia. Not that far away, really. Something like ten hours of straight, hard driving. He's gone lots farther than that. Away from us. Just chasing greenbacks, he'd tell me. Chopping down gold. All for us, of course. Me and Mom. Like he's never had a thought that wasn't right here in this house with us.

An uncle was over last night, the first one since Dad was last here, and I slipped out early, hating those mornings, but when I get home Mom's alone as ever. She's got dinner all ready for me, something reddish-gray and kind of flat. I don't know what it's supposed to be. She eats it, makes a big deal out of it. Me, I don't have those kind of nerves. That kind of stomach. I just watch mine on my plate. Making sure it doesn't get away, not looking Mom in the eye.

She keeps asking about her dinner, asking me to try it— just a bite—but anymore I don't talk to her for days after an uncle's been over. Finally she shoves her chair back and stomps out of the room.

She slams some drawers around, then, next thing I know, she's storming through the kitchen with a load of suitcases. "What?" I say after her. "What now?"

On the next load I grab a bag from her and carry it down to the car. "What?" I ask again, like I'm so tired of packing this way.

"His turn now," she says behind me. "*My* turn."

"What? Whose?"

"Your father," she says, like I've missed something obvious.

"Dad?" My teeth about drop out of my mouth. "We're going *to* Dad?" I try to turn around, get a glimpse of what's going on on her face, but she keeps pushing toward the car.

"What're we doing, Mom? Really?"

We're almost to the gate and Mom lashes out this huge

kick, walloping the hell out of the rickety old fence. Should've landed her foot straight in the hospital, but instead it's the picket that gives, falling clean out onto the patchy grass. "I have spent my last day waiting," she says between her teeth.

"To kick the fence?"

"Wondering which one of us would cave in first."

"You or Dad?"

"Me or that fence."

I wait, but she goes past me to the car. "Are we going to Dad?" I ask again.

"Yes, we are, young lady," she says, holding the door open like it's just some temporary setback we're without a chauffeur.

To Dad, I marvel. I ask if I can drive.

Mom shakes her head.

"It's not just a learner's permit anymore, Mom. I have a real live driver's license."

She snaps, "Aren't you the big girl?" and shakes the door for me to climb in. Once she gets an idea, it's get out of the way or get trampled. The only reason we never sheared that sheep was that the police showed up explaining the differences between residential and agricultural zoning. Bye-bye black sheep.

I slip past Mom into the passenger seat. The blind leading the deaf, Dad would say. But it'll be nice seeing him again. Hear him laughing.

Mom leans in. "Buckle up," she says.

That's when I see the bruises on her neck. Hickeys. On my Mom.

"Mom?" I say, thinking how, maybe for the first time, Dad won't be laughing so much. I didn't even know what a hickey was till I fought my way out of the doofus's car and then, brushing my teeth, I saw this thing in the mirror, thought of his lamprey mouth sucked onto my neck. Mom never said a word about it, though she'd have to have been blind to miss it. Took about ten years to fade away. Mom and me don't have that kind of time now.

"What?" Mom asks, snapping me in like I'm some kind of invalid, or she really is a chauffeur.

I look away from her neck. "Nothing."

Maybe they're fingerprints, I decide. Maybe Uncle got a little rough last night. Maybe that's why we're going to Dad.

Of course, with Mom leading the expedition, we never make it to Dad. We never even get to Canada. Getting close to the border, she wheels into a place alongside the highway, stopping for a bite. "Something to fortify us along our journey," she says, sounding almost like Dad.

But pulling open the door of the gas station cafe she sees the COOK WANTED sign. There's one trucker eating and one skinny guy working. Mom gets hired before I can fake a fit, pull the fire alarm, do anything.

I go back out and sit in the car. I am not stopping here, I swear to myself. Then Mom comes out and drives us around back to the motel rooms. A line of four doors in a building about the size of a railroad car. "This is part of the benefits package," she says to me. "And we can eat in the cafe. Free."

"Mom," I say. "Dad sends us money. We don't have to do this. We aren't at the bottom of the barrel yet. We're still skimming cream."

Mom gets the key in our door. "But won't it be nice standing on our own two feet?" she says, flopping down on the bed, nearly disappearing in the sag of mattress.

I drop beside her. We stare at our feet, dangling out there off the bed. I don't point out that there are four of them.

"Mom," I say instead, "there's only one bed."

"I don't mind. We'll be snug as bugs."

"Pigs in a blanket," I say. Snug as pigs, Dad'd say. Bugs in a blanket.

Mom starts her cooking career that very night. I sit alone on the bed, wondering what the cafe would've done without her. Just closed? I wonder what they'll do with her. When they find out. They might have to close.

The room's the size of a smallish closet. No TV even. I stare at the ceiling. The walls. I wonder how long I'll have to stay here before Mom gets her nerve back to go to Dad. In all the years it's the one thing we've never done. "It's no place for a girl, Mame."

There's a cigarette hole burned in the shade. I pretend maybe it's a bullet hole, that anything could happen here any second. I peer through its tiny circle, spying on the gravel parking lot, the back of the cafe, the Dumpster. Like someone out there might see me if I wasn't so sneaky.

The cafe door slaps shut behind me. "Mom?" I ask. There isn't a soul in the place. "Mom?" I say again, louder. If she ditched me here that'd be the last straw.

Then Mom whirls out from the back, an apron already all dirty around her waist, her hair flying everywhere. No hair nets on the Montana/Canadian border. A billow of smoke follows her out the stainless door.

"Little excitement here," she says fast, waving me back behind the door with her, snagging a fire extinguisher from beneath the counter.

Dad'd be howling. One shift and the place is on fire. I follow, wondering if she heard me calling for her, or if she was just out to retrieve the extinguisher.

The Gravy on the Cake

I'm only a second behind, but it's all over by the time I push past the steel door. Mom and the skinny guy are leaning against a counter, laughing as hard as Dad'd be. There's smoke everywhere, but no fire. The skinny guy's got a tattoo poking out his sleeve. Something with palm trees. " 'Hold on,' " the man says, imitating Mom. " 'I'll get it.' " He can hardly spit it out. He pats her back, then takes hold of her arm, like he's the only thing keeping them both from collapsing on the spot. His fingers press into where she's getting soft, up high above her elbow, and I realize Mom's probably caught a glimpse of the day when heads stop turning her way.

Mom's stamping her foot, patting her hair flat, holding her hand to her mouth. I'm coughing in the smoke myself. "I thought it was water," Mom squeaks out. "I thought that's what it was there for."

Tattoo turns to me. "Oil!" he says. "She pours the oil bucket onto the fire. To put it out!" He's got nice eyes. He's going to die laughing.

"I thought that's what it was there for," Mom says again, wiping her eyes.

"Could've burned the whole place to the ground."

I step from foot to foot, waiting for him to let go of her arm. "Who were you cooking for?" I ask.

They stop a second, still blinking back smoke and tears. "For us," Mom says. "And you."

"Customers been pretty thin lately," Tattoo says.

"Lately?" I ask. Like since the last ice age. And now with Mom cooking, thin is really going to be the rage.

"Honey," Mom says finally, "this is Ron. Ron, Lucy."

Uncle Ron, I think. I glance at the grill, the blackened chips of something, brown-black lumps off to the side, volcanoey-looking. "What were you making?"

"Burgers and 'browns," Mom says, like she's been slinging hash for years.

"House specialty," Ron adds, his eyes crinkling up again. He's definitely a laugher and I doubt Mom stands a chance. Will even put up much resistance. Might roll out the red carpet.

But Dad's still the world's best laugher. It's a cinch seeing what suckered Mom for him when they were both so young, before finding out about his love of postcards.

Ron scrapes the grill clean and starts fresh. He overexplains each step to Mom, who leans back against the counter having a smoke, winking at me, laughing with Ron.

Out in the booth, Ron smashes the last of his hash browns between the tines of his fork, polishing his plate like it's a contest. Catching me staring, Mom smiles, rolls her eyes. Ron slurps his fork clean, sets it on the shining plate, and gives it a spin. You'd hardly have to wash it.

"None of them Biafrans on my conscience," he says to us.

"You're a saint," Mom says. Definite red carpet.

"Clean-plate club," I whisper, something Dad made up when I was little. I watch Mom, expecting that to cattle-prod her or something, but it slicks off her like Teflon.

I wonder if Ron has his own room out in the railroad box motel, if I'm going to have to sleep in the car. "Are you the owner?" I ask. "Is this your place?"

Ron gapes at me, the idea of such success completely beyond him. "Hell, no," he says. "This place is a ticket to nowhere."

Yeah, I think. And you're the driver.

But he starts in then on this restaurant he's been thinking

of opening up in Mexico. On the beach. Lobsters and Coronas. Shrimp and big salty margaritas. Like it's something just anybody might do.

Mom sits up straighter, though, really looking at him now. Outside, Canada's November gales are plinking gravel against the glass door, rattling a loose window, but Mom, it's easy to see, has got the first trace of sea breeze riffling her hair, tropical sun glinting off the ocean chop, blinding her.

"Where?" I interrupt fast. "Where in Mexico?" I wouldn't make any bets this guy could say what direction Mexico is, even if you ruled out east and west for him. "Which coast?"

"Baja, I was thinking," he says too easily. "Pacific side." Then he actually looks at me instead of Mom. "I've been there, honey. I've been most everywhere."

I've seen it on a map and that's as close as I want to get. One long strip of scorched brown dirt. Scorpions. Gila monsters. This guy covered with palm trees.

As soon as my own plate's clean, Mom sends me back to our room. So she and Ron can clean the kitchen, she says. I lock myself in and fall back on the bed, the grease of dinner sitting in me like a lump. "We've got a long day of traveling ahead of us," she'd said. "You better rest up." So I'd have the energy to sit looking out the window?

Just because there is absolutely nothing to do, I fall asleep. Clothes on, bed still made, everything. I turn over once, awake long enough to know Mom isn't back yet. I mean, you couldn't roll over without hitting somebody if they were here to hit. My feet hurt, and I kick off my shoes without untying them, wrestle out of my clothes.

. . .

Sometime later, middle of the night, I wake up with my skin all prickles, somehow knowing I'm not alone anymore, the air in the room around me as close and dark as the inside of a glove. "Hello?" I whisper, though I'm praying there's no one there to answer.

I hear a shuffle, then breathing.

"Mom?" I squeak.

"It's me, honey," she answers.

"Jesus," I gasp, my eyes tearing just in relief.

I hear her steps and she sags onto the bed, rolling me into her. "Honey?" she says again. Usually she just calls me Luce, same as everybody else.

Her hands are on me, feeling around, trying to find where I am. She touches my face, my shoulder. She stinks like cigarettes and booze, which isn't that common, no matter what else she does.

"You okay, Mom?" I ask.

"Honey," she says again, "something's come up. I'm going to Mexico." An odd little laugh burbles out of her. "Can you believe that? Me?"

I try to sit up, but Mom holds me down. "Ron knows this bodega we can pick up for a song. He wants me to cook."

I struggle out from under her. "So he can collect the fire insurance?"

"Now, Luce."

"But listen to yourself, Mom!"

She reaches out, pets my cheek. "Shhh," she whispers. "It's what I want to believe right now. And you're old enough to—"

"I'm sixteen, Mom!"

"I know," she says, still all quiet. "Don't tell me you weren't thinking about leaving. Starting to lay plans."

"I wasn't!" I blurt, before I have a chance to wonder if it's true.

"Sure you were," Mom says. "It's in your genes, Luce. There's nothing you can do about that." She presses her car keys into my hand like a blessing. "I left Dad's address in the car. Directions. There's money there, too."

She breathes heavy for a second or two. Then says, "No, the money's in my purse. Fuck, where's my purse?"

"Mom?" I say.

She knocks something over, searching.

"Turn on the light, Mom. It's okay."

"I think I just broke it," she says. Then cries, "There!" Like it's been a treasure hunt. I hear her purse zip open.

"Maybe you ought to just slide in here, Mom." I scoot over, patting the mattress hard, so she'll hear. "Bugs in a blanket. You know?"

"Don't start talking like him, Luce. I couldn't stand that now."

"But, Mom."

"Luce," she says, "time for you to use that new license of yours. That's what it's for."

"I must have missed that day in driver's ed."

There's a pause, and I hope Mom's smiling. But when she speaks, it's only to say, "I'll catch up with you."

"How?" I blurt. "You're not making sense."

"What does make sense? Cooking here? Sitting home waiting for your dad to blow through?"

"I don't know, Mom, but—"

"No buts, Luce. I've never asked you for anything. Nothing but for you to understand. Only your understanding."

"Mom. Einstein couldn't understand this. NASA couldn't."

She chuckles. " 'If they can put one man on the moon, why can't they put them all there?' "

" 'They faked the whole thing anyway,' " I answer. " 'Was all filmed in Arizona. Built a whole movie set.' "

"Now we're both talking like him," she says, and her breath stutters. "Shit, Luce, don't put me through this."

Something light feathers against my face. I jerk back but I hear Mom fumbling and realize it's the money from her wallet, that she's fishing it out, throwing it at me blind.

"What are you going to do without money, Mom?"

"I've saved some back."

"What am I going to do?"

"You'll be fine. You'll be with Dad tomorrow. We're close now."

"What'll I do when he leaves again? With you off with Tattoo?"

Mom laughs. " 'Tattoo.' He'll like that." Like they've known each other for years.

"Mom, is this about your neck? Did that guy hurt you?"

Mom laughs again, but nothing's funny about it this time. "Shit, Luce," she says. "They all hurt you."

Then, into the quiet dark, she blows out this long, stale breath. "No, honey," she says, "they're just love tattoos. How about that, you got yours first."

That freezes me a second, knowing she knew, and Mom reaches a cupped hand down for my cheek. But she's lost me and she touches my breast instead, a soft, loving caress, cut short as soon as she realizes what she's doing. I've never been touched like that, the doofus too wound up to do anything but yank and pull, like I was some cow he had to milk. I find I can't breathe.

"Jesus, Luce," Mom stammers, standing up quick, the bed bouncing with just me left in it. "I'm sorry."

I can feel myself blushing, here in the pitch black. "Mom," I say.

"He's waiting, honey," she says, cutting me off. And I realize I've been listening to the steady rumble of some kind of big engine the whole time Mom's been in the room.

"I got to go," she says.

"No you don't," I answer, still feeling that last touch of hers.

"Say hello to your dad for me."

"What else should I say to him?" I ask, trying to stab, anything to slow her down.

"Don't get that way, Luce. He'll know what I was coming for. I got a life to find."

"You already have a life, Mom. *We* do."

"Waiting's not a life, Luce."

"I'll tell Dad you ran off with a tattoo-covered fry cook!"

"Come on, Luce," she says like a sigh. "You know what he'll say."

And she's right. He'll give me that big giant hug of his, puzzled, but glad to see me. I'll whisper my news about Mom into his shoulder. Then he'll break away like he does, grinning a little, pulling at his chin. Finally shaking his head. "Ain't that just the gravy on the cake," he'll say. Then he'll swing his arm wide, inviting me into his palace—whatever mobile home or trailer he's in that month.

"Well, what are we going to do with you, Bug?" he'll ask, curious and friendly.

"She said she'll catch up with us," I'll answer, holding out that much for him, trying not to seem too much a ball and chain.

He'll laugh at that. He'll say, "Now what do you suppose the chances are of that?"

He'll give me a second to answer, then say, "About the same as a snowball in a blizzard."

I can see it all clear as day, but then, just as clearly, I catch a glimpse of Dad standing out in the cold of Great Falls with me, pretending he wasn't waiting for Mom to come say good-bye. I remember the way his eyes fidgeted this way and that along the dark street, and, that quick, I realize it wouldn't be Dad saying all those lines of his. It'd be me. Instead of watching him hollowed and trembly without Mom, it'd be me propping him up with all his old smokescreens, trying to make him quick and light again, untouchable by anything we could ever do.

I'll rattle out his mangled sayings like a drumroll just to drown out his quaking, "What will we do now, Luce?"

The only hug I'll really get is the one he'll give just fighting to stand with his legs cut out from under him. Just holding himself up.

"Mom!" I shout, wanting to show her what I've seen, the real Dad at last, but while I've seen the disaster of our whole big, surprise reunion, Mom's snuck back to the door. She opens it quick, a flash of murky light, a quick whispered, "I love you, Luce. I do," then darkness again when she's outside. I hear the truck door open and slam so fast it's practically all one sound. Mom running to keep from stopping.

Left behind, that last whisper fading into the dark, all I feel is the tingling left by her fingers on my breast. I can see why she might want to run for that. Why missing that might make her crazy like it has. But lying back down alone, Mom's car keys still clenched in my hand, I wonder if I'll ever feel anything as good or close again.